A BEAUTIFUL LIE

IRFAN MASTER

ALBERT WHITMAN & COMPANY
CHICAGO, ILLINOIS

Poem on page 28-29: "Where the Mind Is Without Fear" by
Rabindranath Tagore from Gitanjali
Grateful acknowledgement is made to Visva-Bharati University
as the archive holder of Tagore's work

Library of Congress Cataloging-in-Publication Data
Master, Irfan.
A beautiful lie / by Irfan Master.
p. cm.
Summary: In the days leading up to the partition of India in 1947,
thirteen-year-old Bilal devises an elaborate scheme to keep his dying father
from hearing the news about the country's division.
ISBN 978-0-8075-0597-7 (hardcover)
1. India—History—Partition, 1947—Juvenile fiction. 2. Pakistan—History—
20th century—Juvenile fiction. [1. India—History—Partition, 1947—Fiction.
2. Pakistan—History—20th century—Fiction.
3. Fathers and sons—Fiction. 4. Honesty—Fiction. 5. Terminally ill—Fiction.]
I. Title.
PZ7.M423863Be 2012
[Fic]—dc23
2011051132

For more information about Albert Whitman & Company,
visit our web site at www.albertwhitman.com.

For
Ahmed Bhura,
thank you for your stories
&
Gulam M. Master,
we miss you still

Prologue

Everybody lies.

We all do it. Sometimes we lie because it makes us feel better and sometimes we lie because it makes others feel better.

Many years ago I told one lie that has taken on a life of its own. It defines me as a person. The only time I was sure of anything was all those years ago, when I was a boy. When I was lying. Since then I've never been comfortable with anything in my life.

We all do it. On August 14, 1947, I learned that everybody lies, but that not all lies are equal . . .

Anaar Gully, Northern India, June 1947

Chapter 1

Something was wrong. I could sense it but I couldn't put my finger on what it was. It reminded me of when my father would jerk his head this way and that, sniffing the air like an agitated rooster. He would look at me and say, "Can you smell a change in the air, my boy? Monsoon is coming." This feeling was like that. I could sense that there was something on its way but it wasn't rain or monsoon—it was even bigger.

I was walking through the market, cradling a large melon in my arms, lost in thought, but the scent of jasmine tugged me back into the present. I stopped to watch the line of flower vendors carefully stringing petals into piles of necklaces.

Out of all the flower vendors, Jayesh had the sharpest eyes and the nimblest fingers, and his pile was always bundled higher than everybody else's. People from the surrounding villages would come just to see Jayesh sitting cross-legged at his workbench threading flower after flower. I made my way across to his stall. A few months ago he would have had a crowd gathered round but today there was only me. I watched for a few minutes as he delicately threaded each petal without pausing once. I waited patiently for the moment when he slipped a rose petal into his mouth and began to chew—by the time he had swallowed the petal, the necklace would be finished. As he slipped a rose petal into his mouth, I smiled to myself. Some things never changed. But my smile faded as I thought how recently some things *had* changed. It appeared that life continued as normal but there was a tension in the market I'd never felt before; little signs that things were not the same.

My stomach began to growl as I passed the fry cooks who provided food for the army regulars and the Britishers, the daal gently bubbling away in a large stewpot, a huge pot of steaming rice next to it. As I passed another stall, there was the same combination again, daal and rice. I shook my head and walked quickly past. A few months ago, these two stallholders had been partners; one made the daal, the other made the rice, and they split the profits. Their stalls used to be beside each other and they used to sit, as friends do, in the shade sharing the odd cigarette. But that was a few months ago.

As I approached a space shaded by a canopy of bamboo sticks, I could hear a babble of voices all trying to talk at the same time. For as long as I could remember, the elders of the market town sat here spreading lime and betel onto eucalyptus leaves ready to smoke, and talking about the rights and wrongs of the world. My father would often sit here and listen to what the elders had to say, shaking his head at their warnings and listening respectfully as they gave him advice. Now I hung back and stood listening to the voices and watching the gestures of the town elders. I'd always remembered this spot as a peaceful place, where old men dozed or winked at you as you went past or gave you some money to buy eucalyptus leaf, but now it was anything but tranquil. Although a few men still sat and smoked quietly, a good number of the elders were standing and wildly gesticulating. A few others, propped up by their sticks, had stern faces and waited patiently for their turn—not to speak but to shout. One old man actually prodded another with his stick, inciting a few more to stand up and raise their hands in outrage. I walked past hurriedly. The elders had always argued but this was different. It was charged with something else. Something under the surface. Before they had argued and then cooled over a glass of refreshing lassi. Nowadays they stayed angry, feelings festering in the shade. Everything felt askew, like when I put on Bapuji's glasses and everything was magnified and altered. As I remembered how it used to be, I walked in a trance, drifting past Anand's vegetable stall. A sharp sound yanked me back into the present once more when Anand shouted at me.

"Bilal, watch where you're going with that melon! You nearly dropped it on my foot."

The melon weighed heavily in my hands. I looked down at it and suddenly it hit me. Bapuji hadn't really wanted to eat melon. He had wanted me out of the way for when Doctorji came. I quickly handed the melon to a startled Anand and began to run.

Skidding to a halt, I arrived just as the doctor was walking out of our front door. He waited patiently while I frantically tried to catch my breath, doubled over.

"Stand up, Bilal. You'll get your breath back quicker that way."

Breathing in short, sharp gasps, I was unable to speak but stood up, staring intently at his face.

He looked at me closely and leaned forward to straighten my upturned collar, then smiled. "Look at the state of you, Bilal. Thirteen years old and still can't dress yourself properly. How long now since your mother died?"

"Five years . . ."

"Five years is a long time, my boy. You have to take better care of yourself."

"And four months . . ."

"What?"

"And twenty-four days," I replied, looking him in the eye.

Doctorji blew out his cheeks and sighed.

The feeling in the pit of my stomach that I hadn't been able to place suddenly sent little currents of electricity slicing through my body.

"Your bapuji's dying, Bilal. You know this, don't you? You've seen him, you've felt it."

Bright lights flashed in front of my eyes, my entire body tingled. The outline of the doctor's face blurred, making me blink rapidly.

"Bilal . . ." said Doctorji gently.

I forced my eyes to stay open and after a few seconds the doctor slowly came back into focus. Doctorji put a heavy hand on my already sagging shoulder. I felt my knees buckle.

"Your father hasn't long now—a month, maybe two—but we can still make him comfortable. If not for that stroke a few months ago ... If it hadn't left him so physically helpless ... If he could still move and be active, he might have had a chance to fight this cancer." Shaking his head, Doctorji frowned. "Too many "ifs." His mind is strong but his body no longer obeys him. Go to Rajawallah and ask for this prescription. Tell him to see me about payment. You must do that today. Bilal, are you listening?"

I looked at the doctor again and at his hand on my shoulder, then tilted my head to look past him at the gaping doorway.

"Yes, I am listening," I replied, my voice croaky and faint.

"Good. Now you must continue as normal. Keep him in good spirits by going about your usual routine —and that includes school. I have to go but I'll check on you tomorrow. You come to me if you need anything, OK?"

I nodded slowly. Doctorji looked me up and down with his usual stern expression but his eyes were softer, like when he and Bapuji spoke of old times. Turning to go, he stopped and looked back to me.

"And where's that brother of yours?" asked Doctorji.

"He comes and goes . . ." I muttered.

"More goes than comes, I'll bet. Damned fool of a boy, playing at being a man. I'll give him a piece of my mind when I see him, don't you worry. It's no way for an older bhai to behave," said Doctorji, shaking his head and turning on his heel.

I felt as heavy and immovable as an ancient tree as Doctorji marched in the direction of the market. Fixing my eyes on his briefcase, I watched until the black square bobbed out of view. For the first time in my life, I was afraid of walking through the doorway of our home. I closed my eyes and stepped into the darkness.

Chapter 2

Entering the room slowly, I patted the cool, dark clay and leaned my forehead against the wall. It made me feel better, to touch that familiar and solid wall. Bapuji used to say our house was made up of two parts clay, two parts water, and two parts pure goodwill. For me, it was a sanctuary. A place where I knew Bapuji would always be waiting, where he'd have all the answers to my many, many questions.

I knew it was just a mud hut made up of one small space but it was my home. It did have one memorable feature—there was a partition which split the room in two. A partition made up solely of old books stacked floor to ceiling, three books deep. For a while it had been the wonder of the market town community, many of whom had never seen so many books in one place.

After some guidance from Bapuji, I gave tours of our home, pointing out various books and ending the visits by reciting some poetry by Tagore, then bowing and ushering the newly enlightened group out of the front door. Bapuji always said, "Education and literature, my boy, we are all deserving of that. If you have it, you must not deprive others of it." Then he would quote some poetry.

My education started at school but continued at home. Sometimes it was a bit much, having to live with so much knowledge. You only need a little bit to survive. Like where to get clean water or how to mend your clothes, and who you could swap things with to have enough food for the week. Real things, practical things. Nobody would swap books. Believe me, I tried, but the usual answer was, "I can't eat books, can I?" It amazed Bapuji that people couldn't comprehend that letters, words, and books made you richer than you could ever imagine. Even I had difficulty understanding what he actually meant but that was just what he was like. Give Bapuji a good book and he could go without washing, talking, or even eating for days on end.

Bapuji had collected his wall of books over the

course of forty years. He had traded, worked for, salvaged, repaired, begged, and bought each book with a passion that was obsessive. Often, late at night, I'd find him sitting next to the partition in only his dhoti, poring over a book. Upon hearing my scuffling feet, he'd tear his bright eyes away from the page and smile deeply and with such pleasure that it would make me smile too. He'd say, "Come, you must see this," and I'd go and sit next to him, fighting to stay awake as he pointed out strange and wonderful facts about places on the other side of the world or animals I couldn't believe existed.

The air now felt thick as I shuffled slowly into the room toward Bapuji's bed. It was particularly cool and dark on this side of the room since very little sunlight sneaked in through the small window. His low bed was pushed up against the far wall close to his wall of books. I'd spent a lot of time in the charpoi, listening to him reading aloud passages from old books full of strange language that I didn't always understand. I'd often go to sleep listening to Bapuji's voice and have extraordinary dreams about places I'd never been and people I'd never seen. That was the idea, according to him—that through books you could lead a thousand different lives and have a million different adventures.

The pain in my stomach was now a dull ache. I took a breath and pushed it deeper inside. I moved toward the only other piece of furniture in the room, a low stool on which I often sat and read to Bapuji. I picked it up and sat down on it next to the bed.

I watched as Bapuji slept, chest rising and falling in between intervals of ragged gasps and coughs. His hair was mostly gray now, cut short and thinning on top. We shared the same dark-brown eyes, sharp nose, and nut-brown skin. Sweat trickled down his forehead on to his sallow cheeks and clung to his rough salt-and-pepper stubble. He opened his eyes and, not for the first time, I saw how weak and frail he had become. Dark rings circled his eyes and made me think of those pictures of pandas we'd seen in an old encyclopedia.

Bapuji smiled, his face creasing into a hundred little lines. "Fault lines," he called them. "Our very own fractures in the earth's crust." I didn't know what he meant but that wasn't unusual. He tried to sit up, weakly managing to haul himself into an upright position. I sat there tensely but didn't try to help because he hated it when I fussed over him. He propped himself up and looked straight at me with his bright eyes.

"Spoke to Doctorji then, did you?"

"Yes."

"I'll be OK, Bilal."

"I know you will." *Being dead is not OK.*

"You'll be OK too. You'll need to write to your aunt and make arrangements."

"I will, don't worry." *I don't want to live with my aunt. This is my home.*

"It's beautiful in Jaipur and my sister will look after you properly. And the history in Jaipur, my boy . . . I envy you."

"It'll be fine, Bapuji." *I don't care about Jaipur, I don't care about stupid history, and I won't be OK.*

And that was it. No more said. A vicious disease was eating him from the inside out and he wouldn't even talk about it.

"What's the news today, son? Have those vultures come to a decision yet?"

I held myself rigidly because I knew what was coming next.

"Harpies, the lot of them. They just don't

understand, do they? The soul of India can't be decided by a few men gathered around a map clucking like chickens about who deserves the largest pile of feed. They can talk all they want—until the end of time, for all I care—but Mother India will set them straight. Look at your friends, Bilal. Do they care that we're Muslims? We've sat and eaten with Chota's family on many occasions. Are we supposed to hate them because they're Hindus? Take Manjeet—I've known his family since before you were born. I was at Manjeet's father's wedding. They're Sikh, yet we share very similar ancestry and have many things in common. We'll always have differences but our similarities will keep us together. India will never be broken, never be split. Do they think this hasn't happened before? That we haven't been to the brink before? Do they believe India is made of clay and can be shaped according to their petty ambitions? We've suffered this before and will again, but those men— those villains and these visiting British—will never break the back of India. Not in my lifetime, son, not in mine."

Bapuji was shaking with a fury I'd never seen before and his eyes were dark pools of ink that I could no

longer look into. I wanted to scream, "*You're wrong.*"
Only yesterday I had stood with Saleem in the
marketplace listening to the wireless as Nehru–ji had
spoken of the partition plan, of the new world we
were going to create whether we liked it or not. *How
can they do that? Take a map and say, "Here's the line.
Choose which side you want to stand on."* Partition was
like laying flat a piece of coarse material and cutting
it as steadily as you could down the middle. The only
difference was, once the first cut was made, no amount
of sewing and stitching could make that material
whole again.

Bapuji hadn't been out of his room for almost a
month. He hadn't seen the changes in the people,
the atmosphere in the market, the elders arguing
around the market square. There had been trouble
and violence last year, but it had died down and life
had returned to normal for a while. But since the
partition plan had been announced, everything had
changed. There were stories of mobs all over the
country, burning people's houses, killing women
and children, and political parties recruiting young
men to fight and further their cause. India was
succumbing to a cancer, like the one that was eating

Bapuji alive. A disease from within.

A sharp pain in my stomach that had started earlier when I spoke to Doctorji made my stomach cramp in anxiety. I squeezed my eyes shut against the pain. Why couldn't he sense it? Everything was changing, everything was wrong. India was on the verge of disaster! I wanted to scream at him, *I don't care about India or politicians or vultures or anything like that. I only care about you!* Instead I went over to his bed, held him close, and lay down next to him. After a while, I felt him dozing gently and disentangled myself from his arms. I looked at him sleeping so peacefully.

I had kept the partition plan from Bapuji thinking that in his ill state it could kill him. I knew now that the effect of the news would in many ways be a lot worse. It would break his heart.

It was at that precise moment that I knew exactly what I had to do. I decided that no matter what happened or what people said, I would make sure that my bapuji would never know what was happening in the outside world. It didn't matter that people were preparing for the worst and that India was on the verge of something big, a monsoon the likes of which they'd never seen, that, once cleared, would change everything. I swore an oath that Bapuji would die not knowing the truth of what was to come. He would die thinking that India was as he remembered it and always would be. At that precise moment, I decided to lie. I set my shoulders and made to leave the room.

"Bilal," croaked Bapuji.

"Yes, Bapuji?"

"Where's my melon?"

I left the room, salty tears stinging my face as I walked out into the light.

Chapter 3
(75 days until Partition)

The sun shone brightly into my eyes as I left the house, and there they were. My three closest friends. They were waiting for me, heads bowed, standing in a semicircle. I knew they'd have waited for Doctorji to walk past the chai stall and chased him down, so they knew about Bapuji. I also knew that he wouldn't have told them anything but that they'd have worked it out anyway. I didn't want to speak, not really, not right now. I stepped forward to complete the circle and stood looking at my feet.

To my left there was Chota, the smallest of us, but also the bravest. If I told him that the angel of death was coming for my bapuji and we were not to let him take him from us, he would spit on his palms and bunch his fists ready to fight. On my right stood

Manjeet, tall, skinny, and with a bright-orange turban tied tightly on his head. He only spoke when he had something worth saying and I always felt comfortable with him, whether we were talking or not. Lastly, in front of me, stood scruffy-haired Saleem, who many thought was my brother because we were always together. "Joined at the hip, you two," Bapuji would say, and he was right. We were separated only when we had to go home.

We stood in a circle and stared at our feet for a long time. Finally, I looked up and they looked up too. In their faces I saw only the same sadness I'd seen in Doctorji's face. I would need their help if I was to succeed with my plan and fulfil my oath.

There was silence for a while after I'd told them what I wanted to do. I thought they'd try to persuade me it was wrong, but they just looked at their feet. Then Saleem put his hand on my shoulder and nodded.

"We understand, brother. We'll help you."

I didn't know what else to say so we went to our favorite vantage point, a derelict old house now used for storing dried chilies, from where you could see over the whole market. I picked up a stick and started drawing random shapes in the ground.

"You all know how people like to visit my bapuji and give him news," I started.

"That's because he's got the best stories and—" Chota stopped talking when I glared at him.

"Anyway, we have to stop everybody visiting," I said rather sharply.

"What, everybody?" asked Manjeet, who, not unusually, had been very quiet up until this point.

"Yes. Everybody."

"There are other ways he might find out," said Manjeet.

"He likes to read the newspaper," said Saleem.

"He hasn't seen a newspaper for a while so maybe we can put that off," I replied.

"But when he does want to read one, what then?" asked Manjeet.

"Well, we'll deal with that when it happens," I replied, a little flustered, arms folded across my chest.

Saleem, in his usual way, gathered us all into a huddle and put his arm round my shoulder. I smiled at him appreciatively.

"OK, tell us how we're going to do this."

I picked up the stick again.

"Right. Tomorrow, you, Chota, will not be in school," I said, pointing the stick at him.

"Where will I be, then?" asked Chota, confused.

"You'll be on this roof, watching my house to see if anybody tries to visit Bapuji. From here you can see all the streets leading to my front door. The minute you see somebody approaching, jump down and throw a little pebble through the classroom window."

"Then what?" asked Saleem.

"Then either you or Manjeet will create a diversion in class so I can slip out and meet whoever's trying to visit and give them a very good reason why they can't."

Everybody was satisfied with the roles they had to play. Chota was never in school anyway, and that would please Mr. Mukherjee as he tended to fall asleep and snore really loudly. Manjeet and Saleem would play their parts, and I had already thought of a hundred reasons why my bapuji couldn't be visited. I was confident it would work. As the sun went down, we watched the market close for another day. It was the quietest we'd been in a long time.

Chapter 4

The next day started like any other. I put on my well-mended uniform and kissed Bapuji good-bye. He mumbled something I didn't understand and gave me a hug. I collected my books, pens and school bag and made my way to school, kicking stones all the way there. By the time I got there, my toe was throbbing but I didn't mind the pain. The twinge was distracting and made it easier to hide how I really felt deep inside. Mr. Mukherjee was waiting at the door, ushering in all the latecomers, and he hurried me in. I looked over my shoulder and smiled, knowing Chota would be making his way to the rooftop. It was going to be a long day but I was confident Chota wouldn't let me down.

I bumped into Manjeet going into the classroom

and we chuckled conspiratorially and sat down on the mats near the back of the class. Saleem, who was a few rows ahead of us, turned round and winked as we all packed into the little room, shoulder to shoulder. Once we'd had desks donated by the local market traders' association but they'd been stolen last month—though I didn't understand what anyone would want with fifteen desks.

Mr. Mukherjee stood at the front of the class with both his hands raised and we all quieted down.

"Today we will be learning a little bit more about the distinguished history of this land, its poetic past and the works and people that have made it great."

I sighed. This was Mr. Mukherjee's favorite lesson. The greatness of India. Its beautiful past. *Well, what about its beautiful present and future?* I looked up at Mr. Mukherjee, wire glasses wrapped tightly around his ears and perched on the end of his nose, eyes alive at the thought of the glorious past. Mr. Mukherjee wore the same red velvet waistcoat every day with a silver pocket watch attached to a chain tucked into his front pocket. Bapuji thought he was like the rabbit in *Alice in Wonderland* because he was always looking at his pocket watch and muttering. I smiled at the thought and he looked straight at me.

"Bilal, do you find our great history amusing?"

I shifted in my seat. Manjeet elbowed me in the ribs and I elbowed him back.

"No, Masterji, it is a most glorious past," I replied.

"I'm glad you think so. Would you care to come up here and recite some poetry?"

"No, Masterji. I mean, no, I wouldn't mind," I spluttered and stood up.

Mr. Mukherjee loomed over me. His long legs made him tower over all of us and his large, rather rabbit-like ears twitched every so often. He turned to the class and smiled.

"And what shall we have Bilal recite for us today?"

I heard a stifled laugh and then somebody said, "*Aloo Bolaa—Potato Says.*"

Mr. Mukherjee glared at the class for daring to suggest a nursery rhyme and turned to me.

"What do you think, Bilal?"

I looked around our small classroom. There were almost forty of us crammed into this little room. Most of us didn't even have pens, at least half couldn't read without help and most would never finish school. Whatever the glorious past, the present had nothing to do with glory and everything to do with survival.

"Shall I begin, Masterji?"

Mr. Mukherjee looked at me and smiled. He was a kind man and he knew my bapuji taught me at home. I would often stay behind and he would show me pieces of his own poetry and writing. Mr. Mukherjee was the only teacher in the whole town and with the exception of my bapuji he had no one else to talk to about his writing. Despite how I felt inside, I didn't want to let him down.

"Yes, of course, Bilal. Go ahead."

I cleared my throat like my bapuji had taught me before starting any recital and began:

"Where the mind is without fear and the head is held high;

Where knowledge is free;

Where the world has not been broken up into fragments by narrow domestic walls;

Where the words come out from the depth of truth;

Where tireless striving stretches its arms toward perfection;

Where the clear stream of reason has not lost its way into the dreary desert sand of dead habit;

Where the mind is led forward by thee into ever-widening thought and action—

Into that heaven of freedom, my Father, let my country awake."

After I'd finished, Mr. Mukherjee beamed at me in pleasure. "Tagore himself would have been proud of that recital," he said, patting me on my back.

Bapuji had taught me those words almost as soon as I could speak. They had always sounded so beautiful to me. But today the words felt empty with little meaning.

The day dragged on as Mr. Mukherjee decided that we were too noisy and that learning math in the afternoon would calm us down. As he was writing on the blackboard, I heard a sharp yelp to my left and turned to see little Jamal holding the side of his head. I shuffled closer to him and grabbed his arm.

"What happened?"

"Something hit me on my head," he replied, rubbing the side of his head furiously and pulling a sour face.

I started scrabbling around, looking for a pebble, shoving the other boys out of the way. Jamal thought it was a game and jumped on to my back. Seeing this as an attack on me, Manjeet jumped on to his back. However, Saleem, who liked math, was busy concentrating until somebody tapped him on his shoulder and he turned just in time for big Suraj to jump on him, almost squashing him flat. By this time, the whole class had decided that jumping on each other was a lot more fun than learning our numbers and the classroom resembled a pond full of leaping frogs. I was at the bottom of the pile, still looking for the pebble. Suddenly I saw it and wriggled my way out from under the heaving mass.

Manjeet saw me making for the door and nodded. He waited for me to sneak out, then whooped loudly, making Mr. Mukherjee turn sharply. At this point Manjeet smiled and jumped on to Suraj's back, who in turn had pinned Jamal under him. Mr. Mukherjee shouted at the class to stop but by this time there was no controlling all the jumping frogs and I made good my getaway, safe in the knowledge I wouldn't be missed.

I sprinted toward my house and was met halfway by Chota. He was grinning maniacally and pulled up short. We both doubled over, panting like dogs, with our hands clutching our knees.

"What?" I asked.

Chota sucked in large gulps of air and coughed. He'd been smoking again. I shook my head and went over to him and rubbed his back. Eventually he stood up straight.

"It's Rajahwallah, the medicine man. He's heading your way."

I told Chota to go back to his vantage point and started sprinting again. Rajahwallah was still a street away when I caught up with him, jumping in front of him and startling him.

"Bilal! What are you doing?"

I fixed a smile on my face. "Why, I'm coming to see you to pick up the medicine. Remember?"

Rajahwallah looked a little confused and puffed out his cheeks. "I thought we'd agreed that I'd drop the medicine off and explain to your bapuji how and when he needs to take it. That's what I remember."

"No, no, you said that you'd explain to me about the medicine and you told me to come by about this time to pick it up. If you leave it to him, he'll probably forget to take it—you know how absentminded he is." I kept my smile in place.

Rajahwallah frowned then shrugged his shoulders. "Well, I've got a few more deliveries to make anyway. Here it is. You need to mix the powder with water until it's like a paste. Make sure he takes it three times a day. If you have any problems, come to see me." And with that, he turned round and started walking back toward the market.

I dropped the fixed smile and replaced it with one of real pleasure. As I walked back past our rooftop, I saw Chota's teeth gleaming down at me and I gave him a double thumbs-up. He leaned right over the edge of the building to wave to me. He almost fell off but managed to save himself and started grinning again.

My system was working! That's what mattered, and having my best friends helping meant the world to me.

Chapter 5

Later that day, we all met on the rooftop as the sun went down and watched as the last few donkey carts were being loaded up for long journeys back to their villages and towns. This was my favorite time of day, sitting on the rooftop, watching the market slowly winding down, hearing the sounds of the market gradually fading. You could see how quick and efficient the market traders were in organizing all their goods and packing them away. Bapuji had once explained to me that each stall was passed down from bapuji to son and that many of these stalls had been kept by the same families since the market was started over two hundred years ago. I often thought about that. I was only thirteen, and thirteen years seemed a long time to me, so two hundred years was too frightening to consider. I couldn't, wouldn't think even two days ahead at the moment. Last year when Bapuji was well, I had had dreams about the future. Of following Bapuji and being a market organizer. It was the most exciting job. You met people from different places, everybody knew your name, and you were asked to settle disputes on matters of trade, money, and the local community. Bapuji and his father before him had been market organizers and I was all set for being one too.

And now that Bapuji is dying, who will teach me what I need to know? I shook my head to dislodge that thought from my mind but it persisted. *Will I even be here to organize the market? No Bapuji means no "here." Will anybody in this place even remember me in four years, never mind two hundred years?* I clenched my fists as the returning stomach cramps made me double over in pain.

"Bilal, Bilal, are you OK?"

Manjeet and Saleem stood over me, concern etched on their faces. I opened my eyes to see Manjeet's orange turban outlined against the last light of the day. He grabbed my arm and pulled me up.

"I'm fine, I'm fine. Just a little tired," I replied. "Chota, come over here and stop smoking!"

Looking sheepish, Chota stubbed out his cigarette and walked over.

We all squatted down and I unwrapped a package of mangoes I'd swapped with Satram for some pencils. Manjeet produced a small knife and started slicing little pieces for us to eat, though Chota grabbed a whole mango and started sucking one end of it. Saleem clipped Chota's ear and Manjeet shook his head. Chota always loved grabbing things, especially when they didn't belong to him.

"Well, the plan worked like a dream, but what happened after I left?" I asked.

Saleem and Manjeet looked at each other and burst out laughing. Then, without warning, they began to jump on each other. Not one to be left out, Chota placed his mango between his teeth, pounced on the squirming pair, and immediately snagged Manjeet's turban and toppled it. After watching for a few moments, I shrugged my shoulders and joined in, leaping on Saleem. As the sun went down on the market town, anybody watching the rooftop would have seen four grimy, skinny boys of differing heights in a tangle of sharp elbows and knees, giggling like maniacs, entwined in a long piece of sun-touched orange material that bound them all together.

Chapter 6
(69 days until Partition)

My system survived the whole week without incident, although the possibility that Chota would doze off and miss somebody approaching the house worried me. He often fell asleep in class, even when surrounded by jostling, noisy boys. Mr. Mukherjee left him to it. I don't think he knew what was worse—an alert, awake Chota or one who snored his way through a recital of Tagore's poetry.

One evening I told Chota my concerns and he said that I needn't worry; he never fell asleep on the rooftop because there was always something going on in the market—someone shouting, or a conversation to eavesdrop on—and he always had his wood to whittle. From up on the rooftop, you could also see right into the cemetery where they held the cockfights. We all knew the fights were bloody and brutal. Chota's uncle organized the bouts but we didn't have the courage to go to one. Not yet, anyway.

Chota sat in his usual position, perched right on the edge of the rooftop, dangling his legs over the side and chewing on a piece of straw. Leaving him to keep watch, we decided to start up a card game. Wafts of spices and meat in the market drifted up to us. Hesitating over my cards, I heard Manjeet's stomach growl loudly. Saleem rolled about, laughing, and dropped his cards.

"Sounds like you've got a hungry tiger stuck in there, Manjeet!" I chuckled.

"More like a growling tiger cub," chipped in Saleem.

"Laugh all you like but I haven't eaten all day," replied Manjeet, holding his stomach and sighing.

"What about that mango I saw you eating earlier?" asked Saleem.

"And those two chapatis I saw you eat at school?" I asked.

"Don't forget that pomegranate I gave you," added Chota from behind us.

Saleem rolled about laughing, dropping his cards again.

"Well, I did have a few things to eat," admitted Manjeet. "It's your go, Saleem."

Saleem picked up his cards and squinted at them carefully. Then with a big grin he said, "Full house!" He held the cards up so we could all see.

Manjeet looked over at me and made a face.

"Hold on," I replied.

"Saleem, you can't have those cards, your last hand—" Manjeet began.

"What are you talking about? Anyway, you both owe me a mango. I don't mind which variety as long as it's ripe and juicy," said Saleem.

"Wait," I said, looking at Saleem's feet.

"What?" replied Saleem.

"What's that under your chuppal?" I asked.

"When you dropped the cards . . ." said Manjeet, slapping Saleem's foot away and revealing a card.

"Manjeet, sit on him, will you, while I find a bamboo stick to beat him with!" I said, standing up.

Manjeet grabbed Saleem and started to tickle him.

"Aaagh! They must have fallen from the pack. I didn't cheat. Aagh! Stop tickling me, Manjeet, you big oaf!"

Manjeet and I sat on Saleem, with Manjeet

continuing to tickle him.

"Aaaagh, get off me! Manjeet weighs more than a donkey! Get off!"

Laughing, we began to bounce on Saleem, teasing him by getting up and then sitting back down.

Chota suddenly cut us short. "Hey! I think there's something going on in the far side of the market. Shut up for a second!"

Moving closer to Chota, Manjeet and I looked over the rooftops and saw in the dying light a group gathered in a little square near the edge of the market.

"They look like they've covered their faces. What do you think they're doing?" asked Manjeet.

The group were huddled together and were clearly discussing something heatedly.

"I don't know but it can't be good news," I said.

"Let's go and find out!" said Chota, already at the stairs. Before we could stop him, Chota had bounded down the stairs and scampered in the direction of the square.

"That little ... What do we do now?" Saleem asked.

"We have to follow him or else he's bound to get into trouble," I replied.

Manjeet was second off the roof, his long legs carrying him at speed down the stairs. Saleem followed and I was a step behind as we entered the maze of streets. We could just make out a little shape flitting in and out of the alleyways ahead. The benefit of following somebody you knew well was that you knew the route they were likely to take. Anybody who lived in the town knew the shortest route to the marketplace and Manjeet followed Chota unerringly through each twist and turn. As Saleem and I rounded another corner, we crashed into Manjeet, who had stopped and skidded into Chota. Holding his finger over his lips, Manjeet moved us into the shadows.

Whispered voices floated over from the other side of the marketplace. We were still too far away to hear anything. Moving past Chota, I signaled for him to follow me, moving from shadow to shadow. The men had chosen a well-hidden spot and, but for our particular rooftop refuge, we would never have seen them. Behind the marketplace was a small area used for dumping rubbish and unloading goods. Backs tight against the wall, we shuffled along slowly, listening intently as the voices became louder.

"I say we burn it down to make a statement."

"Burning it down is a bit of a strong statement."

"Well, it wouldn't be a statement then, would it, you fool!"

"What if we just broke a few things and messed the place up a little?"

We were within earshot now and right at the edge of the wall nearest the entrance to the square. Chota stood next to me impatiently, trying to crane his head to see round the corner. Holding him at arm's length, I tried to hear what was being said.

"Look, we need to let them know we won't back down. The sooner we can get rid of these Muslim scum the better it will be for us. They're killing our Hindu brothers and sisters all over India. We have to retaliate!"

Eyes widening, I turned to see if I was the only one to hear those words. The shock on their faces told me that they'd heard too and Saleem was signalling frantically at me and trying to grab my hand. Chota managed to escape my grasp and poked his head round the corner.

The voices continued in hushed tones.

"Are you sure we should? I've never started a fire before."

"It's not difficult, is it? You douse a little cloth in oil, stuff it in a bottle, and throw it in. Easy."

"What if someone is inside?"

"As I said, we're here to make a statement. Nothing makes a statement like a burnt, crisp corpse . . ."

Burning someone alive! The thought of it almost made me sick and made my stomach convulse. *This is no place for us.*

Chota ducked his head back in and we all stood utterly still. The voices were barely above a whisper. Saleem was beside himself and dragged Manjeet away a few steps. Holding up my hand, I signaled for him to wait. *If we could just find out who or what they're trying to burn then at least we could warn them.*

Craning my head to hear, I heard muffled sounds almost as if the group were moving away. Feeling Chota squirm behind me, I grabbed him to stop him moving but he continued to struggle in my grasp and I turned to him in frustration just in time to see he was about to sneeze. Holding his nose, I squeezed tight as he covered his mouth and a stifled sound escaped from him. Letting go slowly, Chota smiled and held up his hands. Then, before I could stop him, his head shot forward with a short, sharp sneeze. We all froze. Saleem looked at us in horror as the voices floated over to us once again.

"What was that sound?"

"Who's there?"

I pushed Chota toward Manjeet and Saleem just as we heard footsteps coming toward us.

"Run!" I shouted.

Sprinting, we hurtled back into the maze of streets.

Chapter 7

Behind us we could hear shouted curses and swearing. Turning left then right, we ran toward our rooftop but I realized we couldn't all go there—if we were to escape we had to split up. Chota was in the lead and I yanked his shirt until he stopped. Manjeet and Saleem came to an abrupt halt a few seconds later, breathing hard.

"We have to split up. If we split up, they'll find it harder to catch us. Chota, you climb up to a rooftop the first chance you get and stay there. Saleem, you head in the opposite direction. Manjeet, get away if you can but they didn't sound much older than us so if one catches you, wallop him and get home."

"Are you sure it's a good idea to split up?" asked Saleem. "What about you?"

"I'll be fine. Let's go!"

We all moved out of the shadows and sprinted straight ahead toward an opening. Hearing yells behind us, we split up just before we reached the opening, Manjeet angling right as Saleem sped off to the left. Chota had already disappeared.

I sprinted into the opening, taking a few turns before I stopped to listen for signs of pursuit. Running blindly on would only become confusing and I wouldn't know if somebody was following. Stepping into a shaded alcove, I stopped and doubled over. Gripping my knees with my hands and breathing hard, I looked into the darkness. Straining my ears to hear, I stood up straight and waited. *Nothing. They probably went after the others.* Just as I was about to move out of the shadows, I heard a scrabbling sound and then a voice.

"Where are you, little rat? I saw you duck in here. We saw you split up and your rat friends have probably been caught already. Where are you? I know you're here somewhere. You don't want to be a rat skulking about all your life, do you?" taunted the voice.

Feeling for the wall behind me, I stood tensed, my body frozen. *Think, Bilal, think!*

"Show yourself, little rat, I'm getting impatient. If

you show yourself I might go easy on you but if I have to find you . . ."

The voice had moved away, to the other entrance to my right. I saw my opportunity.

"Come out, come out, rodent. I have some food for you. You've already made this more difficult than it needs to be, and for that I have something you can eat, little rat. I'm going to burn you, see how you like the taste of flames on your tongue . . ."

Without hearing him finish, I shot off to my left toward a dark opening. The maze of alleyways was thicker here and I knew it well. I heard the taunting voice swearing behind me but it was farther away and I knew I'd bought some time.

It's not enough. I still saw where you went and sooner or later I'm going to catch up.

The alleys were deserted now and dark. The voice I could hear, was it in my head or was he right behind me? It taunted me and made me look over my shoulder. Sucking in short, sharp gasps of air, I put my head down and tried to concentrate on staying ahead.

I'll get you, little rat. I'm right behind you. It doesn't matter how many times you turn or hide, I can smell you.

Sweat dripped into my eyes, stinging them. Blinking hard, I shook my head. The sound of my labored breathing was the only noise I could hear, roaring in my ears. Slowing down, my head pulsed, making my vision swim, and my sides felt like they would split if I didn't stop to rest. So I leaned against a wall and waited.

Standing utterly still, my eyes traced each shadow and alleyway entrance for any signs of sudden movement. *Is he here already? I heard his voice, didn't I?* Feeling the need to move again, I slowly turned my back from the wall and took a few steps. *What is that? That noise. It's coming from my right.*

Gulping lungfuls of air, I ran into the dark not quite sure where I was, my eyes scanning the houses and walls for familiar landmarks. Almost falling, I ran hard through the narrow alleys, desperate for a sign.

The voice was in my head again. *Ha! You think you can escape me? Silly rat. This is just a game. I'm right behind you.*

I looked over my shoulder and saw movement in the shadows. Stumbling, I raced headlong into an alley and collided with someone. Falling down in a heap, we both rolled to our feet. I took a step back.

Bunching my fists, I ground my teeth ready to fight. *I won't make it easy for you.*

"Bilal, it's me, Chota. It's OK, it's me, put your hands down."

Stepping toward me, Chota smiled and shook his head.

"Those fools couldn't catch a lame donkey," he said, baring his teeth in defiance. "Come on, let's get out of here."

"Let's make sure Saleem and Manjeet managed to get away too," I said.

Looking one last time over my shoulder into the dark maze, I let Chota lead me out and away, doing my best to ignore the sound I was sure I could hear—of following footsteps slapping the ground behind us.

Chapter 8

Arriving home, I stood outside in the quiet street. Fetching a bucket of water, I splashed my face and tipped it over my head. The cold seeped into my bones. I could feel droplets of water tracing tracks down my body. I pulled my legs in and hugged myself as my skin cooled, making me shiver. It felt good. *You can't burn if you're wet.*

Looking toward our house, the warm light beckoned and felt welcoming. Walking in and closing the door behind me, I felt safe once again. Suddenly, my stomach growled and made me think of Manjeet earlier and how we had been laughing at him. How quickly everything had changed. Moving into the room to check on Bapuji as he slept, I held my stomach. Everything was changed but right here, right now, everything was the same. *Hold on to that. Don't let things change in here.*

My stomach growled again and I decided to cook some rice. It was the only thing Bapuji could swallow easily and keep down but even then I had to force him to eat it.

It was a balmy night and I could smell the different foods being cooked up and down our little street. I could smell the fish Anjum-bhai would be wafting over hot coals opposite our house, and I knew Tasneem-bhen next door would be cooking daal because she cooked daal almost every day, except Tuesdays when she washed her hair. Her husband was always complaining of stomach gas. Bapuji supposed it was because Tasneem-bhen didn't think much of her husband's lack of motivation to work, so she cooked daal as a punishment. Bapuji also pointed out that she usually slept next door with her children at her sister's house, and he held his nose and pulled a face and we both giggled at the thought of Latif-bhai living in a toxic haze.

I loved spending time in the evenings with Bapuji, although these days more often than not he would tire quickly and fall asleep while I read to him. I would try to ignore it when Bapuji stumbled telling a story but he would get upset at the thought that he'd ruined a story or be angry with himself for his memories and thoughts failing him. Now, when he asked if I wanted a story, I would purposely choose a short one so he was able to finish it and then I read to him until he fell asleep. Even so, Bapuji was the best storyteller in the market town and the reason for this—he never failed to remind me—was that his stories had a special purpose: "A story has to settle on you long after the teller has finished. Then, as if a key has been turned in a lock, the door is opened and all that you've learned is before you."

He painfully propped himself up in the bed and let me feed him the mushy rice. Between mouthfuls he asked me questions about the market, about Doctorji, and what Mr. Mukherjee was teaching in class nowadays. He asked if he still wore his silver pocket watch (he always asked that), and laughed when I told him that Mr. Mukherjee still looked at it all the time and muttered to himself. I also pointed out that he had very rabbit-like ears, which almost made Bapuji spill the bowl of rice onto his lap.

I made some hot, sweet chai and sat at the end of the crumpled bed. I swirled the hot liquid in my mouth and took in the evening's events. I wanted to remember this scene exactly as it was and I didn't want my memory to fail. Not ever. Bapuji had told me of the powerful cameras that could take stills of history and time that we saw in books and newspapers and they gave me an idea. If a machine made by man could do that, then so could we. Preparing myself mentally, I blinked my eyes and took some photos. Of the brightness in Bapuji's eyes. Of the smells wafting through our window. Even of Latif-bhai sleeping in his daal-induced fog. I blinked it all in and stored it all away. Bapuji saw me and asked if I was OK. Instead of replying, I asked him another question that had been on my mind.

"What about fate, Bapuji? Do you believe in fate?"

A few days ago in class, Mr. Mukherjee had explained fate as something beyond our control and asked, "Do we have our lives entirely planned out for us already, and if we do, does that mean we should just sit back and let them take their course?"

Bapuji looked at me. It was as if a light switch had been turned on inside his mind. His eyes twinkled like golden rubies in the soft candlelight and he sat farther up in the bed. I could almost feel the energy pouring from him. I squeezed his hand. I loved him when he was like this. Alive and lit, ready to be shot up into the air like a firework.

"Let me tell you a story, my boy. About fate."

Grimacing in pain yet with a look of pure pleasure on his face, this is the story he told.

*

A merchant was taking his morning stroll by the seaside when he saw a man squatting on the beach and filling a cup with sand. As the merchant watched, the man emptied the contents on a large pile of sand beside him and began filling the cup again. The merchant went up to him and asked him what he was doing.

"I am Fate," said the man. "I am measuring out the food each man is to receive today."

"Can you really do that?" asked the merchant. "I challenge you to withhold my lunch today."

"As you wish," replied Fate.

The merchant bought a fish and took it home and gave it to his wife. Then he went on to his place of work. In the afternoon he came home and sat down to eat. His wife placed the cooked fish before him.

Fate said he would withhold my lunch, thought the man, *but now who can stop me from eating this delicious fish?*

And he burst out laughing. His wife thought he was laughing at the way the fish had been prepared and she began to scold him. The merchant grew angry. He got up and stormed out of the house. It was only when he cooled down that he realized the significance of what had happened: Fate had succeeded in withholding his share of food for that afternoon.

*

I waited for the story to settle into my mind, like Bapuji had always taught me. After a few minutes I looked at Bapuji, who was studying me intently.

"I understand the story but then what's the point?"

"What's the point of what?"

"What's the point of trying to do anything? Of achieving anything if it's predetermined? Why does anybody bother?"

However, Bapuji was fading fast so I stopped talking and urged him to lie back down. Blowing out the last few candles, I set a cup of water next to his bed. I stroked his head until I sensed him breathing steadily and went to my cot in the corner. Just as I was about to blow out the remaining candle, Bapuji spoke.

"The point is to live, my boy. Live your life, come

what may, and leave the rest to fate."

I lay still on my cot. Sharp pangs flicked my insides. Curling up into a tightly coiled ball, I willed the pain away. Fate may tinker with other people's lives but not mine, not with me, I decided. I was in control of my own destiny, and I would control events. With that final thought, I closed my eyes and with great care began to sort through all the memory photos I'd taken.

Chapter 9

The next morning, a scrabbling sound made me tentatively open one eye. It was still early and I really didn't want to wake up just then but the scratching sound continued so I opened one eye a little bit more, allowing me to remain half asleep. The sound stopped and, sighing happily, I closed my eyelid again.

A few seconds later, I felt hands on me and woke up with a jolt. Fully alert now, I rubbed my blurry eyes and looked up to see my brother, Rafeeq, in front of me with a finger on his lips urging me to be quiet. He signaled with his head that he wanted me to follow and he tiptoed into the other room. Muttering under my breath, I looked longingly back at my cot before gathering my school clothes and following him out. My brother turning up out of the blue and waking me up so early in the morning was never a good thing.

"What is it?" I growled.

He looked at me, scowled, and produced a little stub of a hand-rolled cigarette and a mangled box of matches.

"You know you can't smoke in here, the books might catch fire. Bapuji would get very upset if he knew. Go outside."

He muttered something under his breath and made to leave. Shaking his head, he suddenly grabbed me by my shirt collar and yanked me toward him, dragging me out of the door while cuffing my head roughly.

"Get off me, you big donkey. Get off or I'll bite you," I said as quietly as I could through gritted teeth.

He spun me round and kicked me lightly on my backside. Lighting his cigarette, he leaned against the house and looked me up and down. Propping myself up against the opposite wall, I did the same.

It had been at least a month, maybe longer, since I'd last seen my brother. He was dressed entirely in white and had a white handkerchief tied tightly around his head. The beginnings of a beard flecked his face but, like Bapuji, he always shaved his moustache off. The sun bathed the front of our hut with a bright light. He smiled right at me, chuckling at my scowl, which according to Bapuji was the replica of his own. I could almost hear my brother saying, "*So serious, you two, so serious. Go and get a lassi and calm down, will you? Life is to be enjoyed not endured.*" I looked at Rafeeq but didn't smile. He looked a lot like Bapuji and I blinked and took another picture, storing it away for later. In case I didn't see him again for another month.

"How's the old man?" he asked, stamping out his cigarette and looking at me carefully.

I looked back at him with a challenge in my eyes, an accusation. *Where have you been? He's dying. That's how he is. Soon he'll be gone. Can't you even visit and sit with him for a while?*

It struck me that it was probably a good thing he hadn't been around. Every time he visited he argued with Bapuji about what was happening in India, about religion and his "new friends." Bapuji called them fanatics—"The worst kind of patriots because their first thought is violence." Dropping my head, I looked down at my bare, dusty feet. It was better he didn't visit after all. Lifting my head slightly, I saw that he was still looking intently at me.

"You must have spoken to Doctorji. You know how he is," I said, almost spitting the words out.

He stared into my face, probing for something. Agitated, he looked away and patted his shirt, searching for another cigarette. He stopped fidgeting and sighed.

"He's dying. I know. Like this damned country. Day by day it's slowly falling to its knees."

He looked at me with glowering eyes that made me flinch. They scalded me with their heat.

"Bilal, soon it's not going to be safe for you here. You have to be careful and get the old man out. Sides are being picked as we speak and sooner or later lines will be drawn. We'll all be forced to pick a side. Can you understand that? We are Muslims, they are Hindus and Sikhs. We might share the same space, buy the same food, and talk the same language but . . . we're not the same."

Sleep still clung to my eyes and I shook my head to clear it. The fury in his voice was terrifying.

"Bapuji will never leave. You know that. Never. You know how he feels about what's happening . . . He . . ."

Bhai scowled at me again and shook his head. "He still believes his precious India will be OK, doesn't he? Look around you, Bilal! Does it look or even feel like the same place to you? It's all different, all changed. Those vultures are circling as we speak. Soon they'll be swooping down to fight over what's left. The carcass of India, picked clean by so-called peaceful men, learned elders, and politicians—our so-called betters. I reject them. It's time for change."

Unable to endure his intensity, I looked away and closed my eyes. I didn't know my brother in that moment. He had the same passion, the same energy, the same unwavering strength as Bapuji. But I felt nothing. I felt empty. He stopped speaking and spat on the ground. I didn't have time for his anger. I'd pushed my anger deep inside, why couldn't he?

"Look, I have to go to school," I said and turned away from him.

No longer angry, he looked sheepish, like he didn't know where he was or why he was there. I made to go past him and he put his arm across the doorway to stop me going into the house.

"I've put some money in your silver tin. I don't know when I'll be back."

Muttering a half-hearted good-bye, I slipped under his arm. Feeling his eyes on my back, I willed myself not to turn round. I heard him turn and march up the street without saying good-bye. Ducking my head back round the doorway, I watched as he disappeared into an alley.

A dull clanging sound broke the morning silence as Mr. Mukherjee started to toll his school bell. Hurriedly, I started to get dressed for school. I couldn't afford to be angry with my brother. The next time he visited, I'd tell him not to come again. It wouldn't do to have him ruining things. I had a plan and I would see it through, no matter what.

Chapter 10
(60 days until Partition)

A typical market day started just before dawn, the rising sun gently bathing the town and the market traders in golden light. As ever, a few donkeys wandered around the edges of the market square munching on bits of straw, and mangy dogs looked for scraps to eat. Somehow, seeing people getting on with their lives made me think that perhaps Bapuji was right. Nothing ever really changes. Major events you read about in the newspaper and heard on the radio were just that. Bigger than you could imagine. They didn't touch ordinary people like me and Bapuji, who just wanted to live happily near a market.

I sprinted past old man Pondicherry, sitting as he always did on a weathered old barrel in the shade right at the edge of the market. He whistled at me and called my name. He was blind as a bat but he always knew when *I* went past him. Sometimes, a few of the other boys and I would sneak up on him and, waiting until we were just behind him, he would turn suddenly and surprise us! He would chuckle to himself and say, "You ordinary people only have a limited number of senses but I have an extra sense which you can't see." I didn't have time to stop so I waved at him and immediately felt like a fool. Glancing back over my shoulder as I ran, though, I saw him wave back at me. I shook my head in bewilderment; he really did have a special sense!

As I rushed to school, I made a slight detour to see if Chota was on the roof.

"Chota! Chota! You up there?"

No reply.

I anxiously shouted up again. Mr. Mukherjee would be ushering in the last of the students and I really needed to get going. Suddenly Chota appeared on the rooftop, a little bleary eyed. I looked up at him, relieved.

"I've been shouting for you. Where have you been? I thought you might still be at home in bed."

Chota rubbed his eyes with a puzzled expression.

"Why would I be at home in bed?" he asked, pulling a face.

I shrugged my shoulders. "Because you might have slept in or not been woken up by your mother, perhaps. I don't know."

Stretching like a cat, Chota shook his head. "Well, there's no danger of that happening, Bilal," he said, yawning.

I shrugged my shoulders, not comprehending what he was getting at.

"There's no danger of that because I slept on the roof. I have done since we agreed to the plan."

I stared at him with my mouth hanging open.

Chota laughed. "Don't you think you should get going? You'll be late for school. I'll see you later." And with that he waved good-bye and sauntered back to his vantage point.

At a complete loss for words, I turned round and sprinted toward the dying tolls of Mr. Mukherjee's rusty bell.

Chapter 11

As we all settled down, Mr. Mukherjee stood at the front of the class looking very pleased with himself. He had his pocket watch in his hand and kept looking at it every few seconds.

"Settle down, everybody, and let's start the day with math."

Collectively, we let out a low groan which hung in the air. Math first thing. Nobody was ever pleased with that except Saleem, who smiled.

"OK, OK, I know, but we do have work to do and if we don't do math now, we won't get a chance again until Monday."

Suraj shot his hand up. "Why can't we do numbers later in the afternoon, Masterji?"

Mr. Mukherjee was almost hopping from foot to foot with barely contained excitement.

"Because, young man, we have a special guest

coming to talk to us this afternoon."

Another murmur bounced around the small room but this time with a very different tone. He had our attention now. I looked across at Manjeet and shrugged. *How special could he be?*

Mr. Mukherjee cleared his throat. "Today, boys, we have an extremely special guest and you must be on your best behavior. If you behave really well, next week we can go to the maidan in the afternoon and play cricket."

This time, a huge cheer reverberated around the packed classroom. *He must be special*, I thought.

Mr. Mukherjee shushed us again and put away his pocket watch.

"This afternoon, we will be visited by Prince Sanangpal Tamar, Crown Prince of Jaisikander and the last remaining heir to a true Rajput bloodline."

A hush settled on the class. Mr. Mukherjee had organized "special" people to visit in the past. Once Bapuji had come, bringing with him an assortment of fruit and vegetables from the market, and Doctorji had visited too, examining a few of us with his stethoscope—but never a prince. We started on our numbers but there was a sliver of excitement in the air.

Sanangpal Tamar of Jaisikander, heir to a kingdom that went back over four hundred years, was a short man dressed in traditional princely regalia with a large, white turban threaded with gold sitting very smartly on his head. He stood at the door waiting for Mr. Mukherjee to announce him, at which point he marched in looking straight ahead and then spun on his heel to face us. Mr. Mukherjee hurriedly pulled up his own chair for the prince, who lowered himself slowly into a sitting position, back straight with his chin jutting upwards. He propped his right leg on to his left thigh and rested his long, curved talwar sword across his thighs. As silence descended around the room, he subtly tipped his head at us in greeting.

"Do you live in a palace with elephants?" blurted out Suraj.

Mr. Mukherjee jumped to his feet and was about to give Suraj a good telling-off when the prince held up his hand to still Mr. Mukherjee, who sat back down and glared at Suraj instead.

"Yes, young man, I do live in a palace but not with elephants. They have their own place of residence. They can be a little smelly to live with."

Even under the watchful glare of Mr. Mukherjee, the class giggled and began to relax.

"Young man, I live in the mountains of northern India, far from here. It's a wild yet beautiful place with striking vistas, valleys, and ravines. The people there are strong, yet hospitable, and will always offer you a cup of cool water and some modest food. They have little to spare but they understand the etiquette of hospitality. My palace overlooks the Kanak Valley and has been the seat of my family for many years. I am the fourth Sanangpal Tamar and the sixteenth prince of Jaisikander."

The class was spellbound. The prince sat upright in the chair and spoke elegantly and clearly about himself and his people. He had a particular way of making you feel as if you were the only person in the room and he seemed totally at ease in our dusty, cramped classroom.

I remembered what Bapuji had said about some of the princes in India's various regions. "Cruel, vain, and corrupt," he'd called them and felt that as long as the titles they held were just titles, then that was acceptable. "They belong to India's past and now it is the turn of the people." *And look how that's turning out,* I thought to myself. I stared intently at Sanangpal

Tamar for signs of cruelty, but he looked like any other man, except that he spoke really well. He also didn't chew tobacco and spit from time to time. His beard was well oiled and his cream kameez was spotless. In the grimy market town we lived in, that was the most impressive thing. I looked down at my shirt and saw a big stain. Rubbing at it only made it worse. Mr. Mukherjee was beaming now and when the prince stopped talking he stepped forward.

"Now, who has sensible questions for the prince?" he asked, glaring at Suraj once more.

It proved to be a futile attempt by Mr. Mukherjee as everybody in the classroom was much more interested in asking some not very sensible questions.

"How many rubies do you own?"

"Not as many as I once did."

"Do you have any tigers?"

"Tigers are not to be owned. By anyone. They are wild and need to be free."

"Have you had anyone killed?"

"Only little boys who asked silly questions," the prince replied with a wicked grin on his face.

Mr. Mukherjee looked around the classroom in horror and when his eyes met mine he raised his eyebrows as if to say, "*Bilal, ask a sensible question. Quickly!*"

Forming a question in my mind, I put my hand up slowly and waited for the prince to spot me through the forest of raised arms. He answered a few more questions patiently then saw me. Pointing, he nodded. I cleared my throat.

"Prince Sanangpal Tamar, my bapuji said that kings and princes are often cruel, vain, and greedy. Is this true?"

Mr. Mukherjee looked as if he couldn't breathe. The prince sat up even higher in his chair and looked right at me.

"This is a good question, young man. Kings and princes have often been cruel, vain, and greedy, but not all are like that. Many care about the people who live on their land and will dispense justice so that any disputes are settled fairly. Their responsibility is to bring trade and wealth to their kingdom so that not only does the royal family prosper but so do the people."

Mr. Mukherjee had settled down and didn't look so red in the face. I put my hand up again and the prince nodded at me.

"But there are no longer as many princes or kings. What can you do now to help the people? What power do you have now?"

A pained expression flickered across the prince's face but he gathered himself and spoke clearly. "It is true we no longer have as much power as we once did. Times have changed, but as long as I have people who live on my land and need my care, I will be their prince. India has changed and is still changing. But the reason I am here today is to tell you this: You are the dream of India. You carry the ideal of this country wherever you go. No matter what happens in the next few years, remember that and hold on to it. I believe in all of you and you must all believe in Mother India."

A hush descended on the class and only the ticking of Mr. Mukherjee's pocket watch filled the little room with a clipped sound. Was India's time running out? I dreaded to think what would happen if the ticking were to stop. As Mr. Mukherjee was thanking the prince for coming, I leaned against the wall and closed my eyes. Princes, politicians, poets, and historians. It made no difference. They only offered words—sounds made to inspire people and give them hope. Lies to make us all feel better for a while. It seemed to me that in a world full of liars, being a first-rate liar was the key skill you needed. Opening my eyes and looking at the prince, I thought perhaps it was the only skill you needed.

Suddenly, I heard a yelp from one of the boys ahead of me. Manjeet bowled into me and we both went down in a stampede of feet and arms.

"What? What's the matter?" I shouted.

He looked at me with a mixture of fear and excitement and pointed to the middle of the room. No words came out of his mouth. I pushed my way through and froze. In front of me not three feet away was a snake. A king cobra! To make matters worse, it was angry and trying to pin one of the boys with its hypnotic swaying. What was a snake doing here and how had it gotten? Then it hit me. Chota. The snake was his diversion! Somebody was on their way to our house. I looked to the window just as a little pebble sailed through. Everybody was frozen in place unable to tear their eyes away from the rhythmic swaying of the king cobra.

I lurched toward the door without looking back. *Can't wait!* I thought and ran out on to the street.

Chapter 12

Chota was waiting for me outside the school.

"A snake?" I cried.

"It's the three holies! They're a few streets away," Chota said, running alongside me.

No! It would be difficult to get rid of them.

We heard stamping feet behind us and saw Saleem and Manjeet coming up fast. Without stopping, we sprinted for my street. Chota and I arrived before the three holies, Manjeet and Saleem hard on our heels.

"What happened with the snake?" I asked them.

"Mr. Mukherjee cleared the classroom and told us to go home. The prince left for a ceremony in the market square," replied Saleem.

From up the street we heard sounds of feet approaching. The three holies consisted of the Reverend James, Pandit Gohil, and Imam Ali. Despite their differences, they were fast friends and would roam the streets of the market town admonishing people for not attending the church, temple, and mosque, respectively.

"Look casual," I whispered under my breath to my friends and turned to face the three holies.

"Blessings on you," said the reverend.

"Assalamu Alaikum," said the imam.

"Namaste," said the pandit.

Smiling, I tried to casually block my door.

"Son, we've come to see your bapuji," said the imam, making to move past me.

"That's very kind of you," I said, holding my ground.

"Yes, prayer will bring him relief," said the reverend.

"I'm sure it will but I'm surprised you haven't heard," I said, leaning against the door.

"Heard what?" asked the pandit.

"Oh, I thought you'd know. It's contagious."

"What's contagious?" said the imam, stopping.

"What Bapuji has. It's very catching. You only need to be there a few seconds and you're likely to get it," I replied.

"Get what?" asked the reverend uncertainly.

"It's flesh-eating . . ." chipped in Saleem.

"First your skin falls off . . ." I continued.

"And then your hair . . ." said Saleem.

"You're welcome to come in, though," I said, pushing the door ajar.

"Perhaps we should come back another time," said the reverend.

"Yes. It might not be a good time right now," said the imam.

"Tell him he's in our prayers," said the pandit, moving away.

Turning quickly, the three holies scampered off down the street and disappeared down an alley. Watching them go, I turned to see Chota, Manjeet, and Saleem rolling around on the ground, holding their stomachs with laughter.

"I've never seen them move so fast," said Saleem, tears in his eyes.

"That was very funny," chuckled Manjeet.

"I don't know whether to laugh or cry," I replied.

Chapter 13

The market town had had a fair share of royal persons visit in the past but it was always an occasion when they came. I'd imagined that even in these strange times people would be excited and happy that the prince was here but instead I could sense a tension in the crowd.

I moved closer to the circle of people surrounding the prince and elbowed my way to the front. The town mayor was speaking to him animatedly and the talk was turning to politics. The prince looked bored and he caught my eye. He whispered something to his man-servant next to him and pointed in my direction. I looked behind me to see what he was pointing at and turned to see the big man stop in front of me. He looked me up and down and thumbed in the direction of the prince.

"The prince wants to speak with you, boy. Come with me."

Feeling a hundred eyes on me, I involuntarily took a step back but somebody in the crowd behind shoved me into the manservant's arms. I turned to glare but was quickly ushered toward the gathering of elders and committee members. The prince was sitting on a chair over which a square of azure material had been draped. His talwar still rested over his thighs. He finished talking with the mayor and then turned his attention to me.

"How are you, Bilal? I enjoyed visiting your class today. I've found that all over this land there are bright boys just like you."

I mumbled thanks and looked at my feet while another man came and rather vigorously shook the prince's hand. Looking out into the crowd, I saw mostly grim faces. *Something doesn't feel right.*

"We don't need any more princes," said a voice in the crowd.

"Go back to your kingdom, prince. The people don't need you anymore," shouted another voice.

"Let the people govern themselves."

"You're bleeding the people dry . . ."

The crowd was becoming boisterous and began to push forward. Standing up, the mayor held up his hands and asked for calm but was drowned out by the shouting. The big manservant stepped in front of the prince and put his hand on his hip. He was wearing a long coat. *Does he have a revolver?* Other members of the committee now also stood up. Glancing around nervously, I noticed there was an alley behind us. From the other side of the square I could hear tramping feet and whistles. *Police.* The crowd was really pushing forward now and the prince's manservant reached under his coat.

"Wait!" I shouted. The prince turned to me and stayed his manservant's hand.

"What is it, Bilal?" he asked.

"I can get you out of here. Don't shoot anybody," I replied, looking at the big man.

The police were almost here and in a few seconds it was likely to turn ugly. The prince weighed up the situation and stood up.

"OK, young man. Lead the way but we will not run," he said calmly.

With the manservant covering our retreat, we walked into the alleyway just as the police arrived, diverting the crowd's attention. Walking briskly, I composed myself as Bapuji had taught me to do and waited for the prince to talk.

"We are in your debt, Bilal. I have heard many good things about your family from Mr. Mukherjee and about the work they have done to make this market town so successful. I have also heard that your bapuji isn't well, which I'm very sorry to hear." He looked straight at me when he said this and although I tried to meet his gaze, I couldn't. Instead I blurted out the first thing that came into my mind.

"He's dying. I'm supposed to carry on the family tradition but he won't be around to teach me what I need to know."

"I am truly sorry that your bapuji is dying, Bilal, but you will learn what you need to know all the same."

"How? He knows so much, more than anyone I know." The prince looked sideways at me and smiled.

"My own bapuji died suddenly when I was fifteen years old. I was shocked—we all were. He was so strong, so energetic. I thought he would live forever but just like that he was gone. No good-bye. Nothing. I went from playing with my wooden soldiers to ruling a kingdom and being married all in the space of a week."

It was my turn to look at him. "It was a confusing week then," I ventured.

He threw back his head and laughed. "Incredibly confusing! All I wanted to do was play with my wooden soldiers but instead there I was ruling a kingdom. I hated my bapuji."

I looked at him in surprise. *Hate?*

"I hated him for leaving me, for making me take on a responsibility I wasn't ready for, and for not being there to teach me what I needed to know."

I didn't hate my bapuji. I couldn't hate him, no matter what. But he was leaving me and I needed him more than ever and he wasn't going to be there.

"Do you still hate your bapuji?" I asked.

"No, and I realized that I'd never really hated him. I had learned what I needed to because I had to and because I was his son." We stopped walking and he turned to face me. "You will too—because you have to and because you're his son."

I nodded my head and forced a weak smile. We continued walking until we were far from the market square and had found a shaded alcove in which to sit. The prince sent his manservant to fetch some cold drinks.

"Your bapuji, he sounds like an extraordinary man and I'd like to meet him. Do you live nearby?"

My stomach lurched and I stood up far too quickly. All the blood rushed to my head, making me stagger. The prince set me down and waited for me to recover.

"Bilal, what's the matter? At the mention of your bapuji, you turned pale. What is it?"

I waited for the spots in front of my eyes to subside and blinked my eyes rapidly. The prince stood over me looking both concerned and confused.

The prince lives miles away. It doesn't matter if he knows, does it?

In the next instant I'd told him everything. About the oath and the system of deterring people from visiting and how determined I was to make sure Bapuji never found out the truth. The prince paused momentarily and wiped his brow with a handkerchief. I gathered myself and looked him straight in the eye but whereas before there had been strength and resolve in the prince's eyes, now there were tears. I looked away quickly in case I embarrassed him and inwardly cursed myself for being such a big-mouthed fool.

"Bilal, no one should have to take on this burden. Will you not reconsider? The truth may give him peace."

"No," I said firmly and shook my head.

He looked at me again then nodded.

"I wish I had your courage, Bilal. I'd still like to meet your bapuji. Don't worry though. Your secret is safe with me."

I nodded. The big man came back with the cold drinks and we set out. As we turned the corner, Manjeet, Chota, and Saleem were already there, nervously loitering outside my front door. They'd obviously seen me from the rooftop, unable to guess what was going on, but they were still here standing with me, no matter what. My heart jumped knowing they were my friends. The prince smiled at them.

"So these must be your eyes and ears, Bilal? A steely-eyed bunch, if ever I saw one." Turning to me, the prince said, "I'd like to talk to your bapuji alone. Please trust me."

I looked at Saleem then Manjeet and Chota, then turning back to the prince, I nodded my head slowly. "I trust you, Prince," I replied and opened the door.

When the prince reemerged, we all stood up and I approached him nervously, my heart rattling like a drum.

"He is very feverish and couldn't talk for long but what a memory he has! Such knowledge and curiosity set any man apart—and any boy," he said, smiling at me. "I sang him a song my mother used to sing to me when I was a child, about the Himalayan peaks and the ascent of the lords of the high rises, the majestic eagles. I hope it gave him peace for a little while. He also spoke about you, Bilal, and confirmed for me what I have already learned about you in such a short time. I must go now, child, but you have reminded me of a few things I thought India had lost."

Handing the talwar to his man, the prince positioned himself in front of us and bowed gracefully, his turban almost touching the ground. We all shuffled our feet, confused as to what we ought to do in return, but Manjeet stepped forward and returned the bow which, if not as graceful, was a good attempt. Chota almost fell over in his attempt to bow but righted himself with Saleem's help. The prince and the manservant watched us, big smiles on their faces. Blinking my eyes, I took another photo—of the strange sight in that narrow street of a prince bowing, dust swirling around us.

Chapter 14

I promised to meet Chota on the rooftop later and went to see if Bapuji was still awake. The darkened room always soothed me and I grabbed my stool and set it down next to Bapuji's bed. He looked as if he was dozing but I couldn't be sure so I leaned in close to listen to his breathing.

"Boo!" He sat up suddenly, almost making me jump out of my skin. "Ha! Got you, didn't I?"

"You really did, Bapuji. Just take it easy."

"Bah. I've had enough of taking it easy, Bilal. I need some excitement to keep this heart ticking."

He slipped me a sidelong glance. I sighed. He clearly wanted to say something but was waiting for me to speak. Smiling, I folded my arms across my chest. I knew what was coming next.

"What?" I asked, grinning.

"What?" Bapuji said, rolling his eyes exaggeratedly and throwing his arms in the air. "A prince of

Jaisikander visits me and sings me an old song of the eagles and the mountains and you say *what*? Ha!"

Shrugging my shoulders, I shoved another pillow behind his head. I felt his forehead with the back of my hand and he caught me frowning.

"Stop your frowning, Bilal. Now, tell me where and how did you meet a prince and how on earth did you convince him to visit me?"

"OK, I'll tell you the story if you promise to take your medicine now and lie back down. You're burning up, you know."

Bapuji sighed and signaled for the medicine. I quickly moved to get some water with which to wash it down. He made gurgling sounds as he reluctantly drank the medicine. I made sure he drank one more spoonful while he glared at me but he then visibly relaxed and settled into the pile of cushions. Bapuji loved the ritual of storytelling almost as much as the story itself so I made sure to take my time using all the tricks he'd shown me—dropping in dramatic pauses and exaggerating some of the actions, filling in the gaps with colors, sounds, and smells. Bapuji closed his eyes and rocked ever so gently, a little smile lifting the edges of his mouth. I finished the story and went to refill the glass with some water. I hadn't realized how thirsty I was and I drained the glass and sat back down. Bapuji struggled to keep his drooping eyes open. The medicine worked extremely quickly.

"The prince spoke of you. What did you say to him?" asked Bapuji.

"Just the usual, you know, about the market and us. I may have mentioned Grandfather a few times but nothing else."

I began to fuss around the bed making sure Bapuji was covered properly. He narrowed his eyes but the medicine was taking effect and any suspicions he might have had were fading fast. Closing his eyes, he began to breathe deeply.

"He was very impressed with you, Bilal. If I didn't know any better, he'd snatch you up and take you away to work in some far-off kingdom. Would you like that?"

I watched his face and stood up.

"Is that what you spoke about? Me going away?"

Bapuji opened one eye slightly and pulled a face. "Now, now, you only just stopped frowning—there's no need to start again. We were only talking. He was so impressed with you I just thought, you know, that you could make a life with him."

The room was spinning and I had to steady myself. *What on earth is he thinking? I won't leave here. How could I?*

"Why? I don't want to go anywhere with anyone. My whole life is here. This is where we come from, isn't it? You, Ma, Bhai, and me."

Bapuji turned to stare at his wall of books. He slid deeper into the bed and pulled the covers closely around him.

"I wasn't trying to get rid of you, Bilal. He was so impressed with you, I just thought . . . or I didn't think." Bapuji smiled sadly. "It's hard to think at the moment."

Sighing, I settled back down on the stool.

"You know Grandfather always said you acted first and thought later . . ." I teased.

Bapuji made a face and pretended to look outraged. "You're lucky I can't move, else I'd have cuffed your ear by now."

Lifting the covers I slid in next to him, attaching myself to his arm. He pushed the hair from my face and began gently stroking my hair. In the next instant I was asleep.

Chapter 15
(49 days until Partition)

It was a long time since we'd played cricket and Mr. Mukherjee was reminded of his promise at least ten times a day by ten different boys, so the following Tuesday he announced that we were to play that afternoon. The build-up to a cricket match was always boisterous with notes in barely legible writing being passed around the classroom about the batting order and who had put themselves forward to bowl. This would of course be hotly disputed and the notes would be circulated with more urgency, each time collecting insults and threats as to what would happen if so-and-so were to bowl, and so on.

Manjeet nudged me and slipped me a note from Saleem, which said: *What about Chota?* Chuckling, I shook my head. It was amazing how many times Saleem and I thought the same thing at the exact same time. The thought of Chota spending too much time on the roof was worrying me even though he appeared to be happy. We visited him every day after school, bringing him food to eat and relieving him to go home to see his family. Stubbornly, he would try to convince us that nobody at home actually noticed whether he was there or not but we still made him go. Saleem turned round, pointed to his chest, and mouthed, "I'll do it." I nodded in reply and settled back down. Saleem didn't like playing cricket anyway and could sneak off when no one was looking.

Mr. Mukherjee held up his hands and asked for silence. He had a quick look at his pocket watch and smiled.

A loud cheer erupted from our little classroom.

"OK, boys, it's time. I need some volunteers to carry the bats and wickets. I'll bring the ball."

Twenty hands shot into the air and Mr. Mukherjee picked a couple of boys from the front. He seemed even more nervous than usual. I slid next to Saleem and nudged him.

"Mr. Mukherjee doesn't look very happy, Saleem. Can you guess what I'm thinking?"

Saleem looked at me and shook his head. "Not unless you're thinking about the ripe mango I hid on the roof last night that I just know Chota will have found and eaten." He pulled a face and scowled.

"I'm being serious, Sal. I don't feel good about this cricket match."

Saleem smiled but it wasn't one of his usual smiles. There was concern in his eyes, though he hid it quickly. He nudged me playfully and pointed at Mr. Mukherjee.

"You always worry so much. You're more like Mr. Mukherjee than you know. Always nervous about what's going to happen next. What about right now, Bilal? Let's have fun now and leave tomorrow to, er . . . tomorrow."

I tried to suppress the unease I felt. It was hard to tell with Saleem if he was worried, scared, or even the slightest bit nervous. He always appeared happy and always remained calm. I envied him that.

We trooped out of the classroom in a big crowd despite Mr. Mukherjee's best attempts for us to file out in pairs. He followed at the back of the group, trying to keep us in some kind of order by waving his arms and loudly reciting the rules of etiquette when outside the classroom.

We arrived in a flurry of noise, kicking up dust, our

voices joining and merging with the constant chatter of the market. I noticed Mr. Pondicherry sitting on his barrel in the shade smoking his pipe. Checking to see where Mr. Mukherjee was, I strolled over to say hello. He looked up and smiled.

"Ah, Bilal. How are you, child?"

Throwing my hands in the air, I shook my head in amazement.

"How do you do that, Mr. Pondicherry?" I asked and sniffed my shirt. "Is it the way I smell?"

Mr. Pondicherry threw back his head and let out a long and wheezy laugh.

"I can't reveal all my secrets, can I? Are you all here to play cricket again?"

"It's our reward for being good, or something like that." I kicked a large stone against the wall and shuffled around.

"Stop bothering that damn stone, Bilal."

I looked up at him and frowned. Mr. Pondicherry turned his sightless gaze on me as I continued to nudge the stone at my feet with my toe. It felt odd looking at Mr. Pondicherry because I knew he was blind. His world was dark, yet I never felt he wasn't able to see. If anything, he saw more than everybody else. Looking down at the jagged stone on the ground, I glumly thought that some things weren't really worth seeing.

"I can sense your unease, Bilal."

How can he always sense how I'm feeling?

"Bilal, you have something you need to get off your chest. It's not good to hold on to such burdens, son. Visit old Pondicherry later and I'll see if I can lighten your heart with a story."

"I'll come soon and I'll keep an eye out."

Now it was Mr. Pondicherry's turn to frown.

"And pray tell me what you'll be keeping an eye out for?"

I bent down and picked up the stone and squeezed it in my hand. The sharp edges bit into my flesh.

"Trouble, what else?"

Chapter 16

It was the hottest time of day and the maidan off the market square was mostly deserted. Only madmen and a few soothsayers sat talking to themselves in the bright glare of the sun. When I'd asked Bapuji what the difference was between a madman and a soothsayer, he'd replied rather cryptically that "many argue there's no difference." I shook my head at this and wondered at my bapuji's ability to always be mysterious and never give me a straight answer about anything.

All around the dusty maidan the market continued to thrum with activity. A cricket match was often a welcome respite for the traders from the rigors of selling and shifting goods to and fro but I noticed something right away. The air felt charged with a sort of electricity I'd never sensed before. I stood still and scanned the stalls around me. I had to blink as the number of stalls, colors and smells hit me in a rush. Shading my eyes to adjust to the sunlight, I focused on a few stalls that were immediately familiar. Anand stood at his fruit stall looking over his wares. I blinked to make sure it wasn't a hallucination. *Anand never stands.* He constantly moaned about his aching knees and had had a stool made especially to support his considerable bulk. A few stalls down, Sandhu sat deep in the shade watching over his spices and seeds. I could just make out his red turban, which in the deep recess of his doorway looked blood red. Next to his foot rested a long and gnarled stick. *Sandhu never sits.* He was always moving around making people laugh as they passed his stall, and I'd never seen him with a stick. My stomach convulsed in a series of jabbing pains that made me grind my teeth. Glancing toward our rabble, I could see Mr. Mukherjee still struggling to organize two teams.

Saleem strolled over. "We'll be lucky to get a game in before sunset at this rate." He saw my face and stopped. "What's the matter, Bilal? What's happened?"

"Nothing's happened. Yet. Can't you sense it? It's different around here—Anand is standing and Sandhu is sitting! It's all upside down."

Saleem frowned and moved past me. "Go and enjoy the game. I'll get Chota and send him down. I hope he hasn't eaten my mango, the little thief."

Saleem left and a minute later Chota flew past me giggling like a maniac. I turned round to see Saleem on the rooftop swearing at the top of his voice.

"I ate his mango. Come on, before he starts chucking stones at me!"

I waved to Saleem and jogged with Chota into the glare of the afternoon sun to join the play. Manjeet stood at the crease, grinning. Even without the turban giving him a few extra inches he was the tallest in our class. I'd never seen Manjeet in a shirt or a pair of trousers that actually fit his gangling frame. Manjeet's mother always complained that she made clothes to fit him one day but by the next morning they were already too small. The sun glanced off his orange turban as he hit yet another ball into the sky high over our heads. One of the key factors in winning was to have Manjeet on your side because once he stood in front of a wicket you couldn't see round him or past him.

The field had been set out after a lot of wrangling, a few arguments, and finally a shouted rant by Mr. Mukherjee, who had threatened and cajoled both teams into starting. I watched Suraj standing a few feet away from me, sucking on a mango. *He always has food with him.* Noticing I was watching him, he looked over and offered me a little bit of the pulpy mango he'd been chewing on. I held up my palm to say no thanks and heard the heavy thud of bat on ball. Turning quickly toward the crease, I tried to spot the ball and relaxed when I saw it had been hit in the opposite direction. Looking across at Suraj again, I noticed he had sat down and was now slowly peeling a banana.

I had positioned myself near the market end of the maidan and could hear some of the talk among the stallholders. Only snatches of conversation filtered through to me but there was something about the flavor of what was being said that made me feel anxious. The taste was bitter, like when you ate a bad mango and it tasted really sour but you had bitten into it thinking it would be sweet. A lot of the people had expressions on their faces as if they'd just had a taste of bitter mango. They looked decidedly uncomfortable and nervous. A few shuffled their feet and one or two looked as if they were ready to bolt. Manjeet thwacked another ball far to my left, giving me the opportunity to casually turn round again and look at the market. Now I noticed people standing around in groups and although there were people milling about everywhere, anybody who knew the market could see that standing in a group meant something.

I turned away from the scene, moving toward Mr. Mukherjee on my left. He had also positioned himself quite close to the edge of the maidan and stood rigidly as Manjeet prepared to face another delivery. Shaking my head to clear it, I tried to focus on the game. Vickesh was up next to face Manjeet and he was one of a very few who actually could bowl. The only thing was, Vickesh often thought it was an international test match as opposed to a friendly game in a dusty maidan. He would measure out his approach carefully, counting each step with the utmost care. When he was ready he would lick his forefinger and test the wind. Only then would he nod at Mr. Mukherjee to let him know he was ready. Approaching at speed, Vickesh's first delivery almost toppled Manjeet's turban. Holding up his hand, he mumbled his apology: "Sorry, still finding my range."

Adjusting his slightly skewed turban, Manjeet glared

at Vickesh and gripped his handle, furiously thumping the ground with the bottom of the bat. The next delivery was a bit more sensible and a lot slower and Manjeet promptly dispatched it high over our heads into an alleyway beyond our modest pitch. Chota flew in the direction of the ball, barging into the other boys, then disappeared into the alley. The game came to a standstill as at least ten people, including Mr. Mukherjee, began to look for another ball.

Knowing how long it would take to find one, I walked over to a shaded part of the maidan and sat on an upturned crate. Stretching my neck to look at our rooftop, I tried to spot Saleem but the sun was obscuring my sight and I turned back to the market. As my eyes readjusted to the sunlight, I saw a small group detach itself from the edge of the market and briskly walk toward another group near Anand's stall. I stood up for a better view but there were too many people milling about and I couldn't see what was happening. Skirting around the edge of the maidan, I moved toward the two groups. Just as I was about to approach the entrance of the market, a stick appeared from out of nowhere and stopped me in my tracks. Pulling up short, I took a step back in surprise. Mr.

Pondicherry sat on his weathered barrel looking at me curiously with his sightless eyes—or rather, not looking.

"Pondicherry-ji, I didn't see your stick there," I stammered as the stick held me steady.

Shaking his head, Mr. Pondicherry stood up gingerly.

"That's because it wasn't there until you decided to go past, Bilal. Is this how you keep an eye out for trouble, by running toward it?"

Craning my neck to look over the crowds, I turned back to Mr. Pondicherry and sighed. It was no use lying to the old man—his magical sixth sense sniffed out a liar at ten paces.

"I was just curious," I said, shrugging my shoulders.

Mr. Pondicherry leaned heavily on my shoulder and sighed in return.

"Just like your bapuji. What's made you so jumpy?"

I climbed onto the barrel and looked at where the two groups had now met and were exchanging what seemed to be heated words. Describing the scene to Mr. Pondicherry, he nodded his head in understanding.

"Been happening a lot recently with those two groups. Young boys full of anger, working themselves up in dark alleys and then gathering here for a confrontation in full view. Your brother is with one of these groups, isn't he?"

Grimacing, I nodded my head and mumbled an incoherent reply. I could see Mr. Pondicherry staring at me from the corner of my eye and I jumped down to stand in front of him. He faced me and prodded me with his finger.

"I'm not judging, boy. These are strange times. Your brother always was a hothead, quick to temper." He shuffled back to his barrel and perched on it, laying his gnarled stick across his thighs. "It's only words at the moment. Let's all pray that's where it stays—here in this place at least. How's your bapuji holding up?"

"Fine, he's fine. I'll tell him you asked after him."

Mr. Pondicherry growled at me. "Ha! Can't lie to old Pondicherry, boy. Go back to your game and come to see old Pondicherry soon."

Twisting my neck again to see what was happening in the market, I almost crashed into Mr. Mukherjee, who had noticed me talking to old man Pondicherry and had come across to find out what I was up to.

"Bilal, what are you doing?"

"Nothing, Masterji, just fielding. Mr. Pondicherry called me over, sir."

Mr. Mukherjee folded his arms and raised his eyebrows.

"Oh, and how did he know that it was you he was calling?"

I cursed inwardly and made my face into a mask.

"Well, he didn't call me actually, he just heard some shuffling and called out. I thought he might have been in distress so I went over to see if he was OK."

Mr. Mukherjee unfolded his arms and pursed his lips. Sighing, he put his arm around my shoulders and started walking me back to the maidan. A ball had been found and the match looked set to continue. Not surprisingly, Chota still hadn't reappeared. It was quite a task trying to keep up with Mr. Mukherjee's long stride and I found myself jogging along to keep pace while he muttered to himself and looked at his pocket watch. This was the closest I'd been to his watch and I almost gasped at how beautiful it was. Engraved silver framed a white watch face, blocky Roman numerals with intricate hour, and minute hands delicately keeping time. Mr. Mukherjee saw me staring at his watch and deftly slipped it back into his waistcoat pocket.

"You've been acting strangely recently, Bilal. You and your friends. It's something we need to talk about because it appears to me that something is bothering you, and that in turn bothers me."

"I'm fine, Masterji," I said, looking him right in the eye.

"You and I will have to talk. Soon." I knew he was serious because he lifted his right eyebrow and shook his head.

Vickesh was ready to bowl and Mr. Mukherjee signaled for him to continue. Unable to beat Manjeet with a fast bowl or decapitate him with a head shot, Vickesh delivered a much slower ball enticing Manjeet to hit out wildly, which he promptly did. The ball arced high into the air and straight into the hands of Jaghtar.

"Out!" Vickesh screamed and started to celebrate by spinning around like a dervish.

Manjeet, looking disgusted with himself, trudged off the pitch to sit with his team just as Chota appeared behind me in a rush.

"Where have you been, Chota?" I asked, nudging him.

Grinning, he produced the ball in one hand and a pomegranate in another.

"The ball bounced on to a rooftop so I had to climb up the side of a house, but a girl saw me through a window and screamed and sent her brother out to catch me. He was fat and slow and couldn't even catch a lazy ox!" Looking pleased with himself, he produced a small knife and cut the pomegranate in half. "Oh, and I also stole this from Anand's stall. There were lots of people hanging around there and nobody noticed me. I could've taken anything I wanted, Bilal, but I was good this time."

Folding my arms, I looked at him in wonder. He was small and very slight but you'd never think of Chota being weak or helpless. His white shirt came down to his knees and his black trousers were torn and had a back pocket missing. Picking out the pomegranate seeds with his little knife, he stuffed his round face until he realized I was still standing right in front of him, frowning.

He shrugged his shoulders and offered me a handful of seeds, saying, "You look like Mr. Mukherjee when you make that face."

I self-consciously unfolded my arms and tried to

cuff Chota around the head but he was already off, whistling and holding the ball aloft in a clenched fist like a returning hero. He then rather grandly announced that he'd brought pomegranates for everyone. I then watched as he produced five pomegranates from his pockets!

Once all the pomegranates had been consumed, the cricket match recommenced and I noticed that the mood was lighter. Some of the stallholders came to watch, and as the sun began to dip we had a small audience. Vickesh—with little or no help—had managed to bowl out most of Manjeet's team and now it was our turn to bat. Vickesh and Jaghtar were both raring to go and walked out toward the crease like two international cricketing stars, swinging their arms windmill-like and feinting blocks and off drives in preparation. The small crowd, admiring their confidence, clapped them on to the field and I breathed a sigh of relief that things felt a bit more normal. The sun dipped low over the rooftops and the maidan became a shaded place where people came to walk and unwind.

Grabbing a bat, I made a few feints myself, much to the amusement of my team, who sniggered at my clumsy attempts. Laughing, I put the bat down and began to wonder where Chota was now. Being awful at cricket was fine by me even if it meant batting last and nobody expecting you to survive more than a few balls. I'd never managed to get the hang of swinging my bat before the ball bounced. Manjeet had, on numerous occasions, tried to explain to me that preparation was everything, but it was lost on me. I knew the shot I wanted to play, I could even visualize it in my mind, but by the time I'd done all that thinking the ball had passed me, leaving me frustrated that the world I lived in wasn't the world where I was actually good at cricket.

Vickesh and Jaghtar were putting on a good show for the crowd and were slowly chipping away at the total Manjeet's team had set. Standing up to get a better view of the pitch, I suddenly felt two hands over my eyes and smiled.

"Saleem, I can smell your grubby hands a mile away."

Saleem shoved me playfully and went to sit down with the rest of the team, beckoning for me to follow. We sat in silence for a few minutes, listening to the thud of wood each time Vickesh or Jaghtar batted away another ball. From the corner of my eye, I could see Manjeet limbering up and wondered if he was still fuming about Vickesh trying to take his head off. Saleem sat next to me, paring a piece of wood and watching the game. His sense of contentment was infectious and always put me at ease. They all did—Manjeet and Chota, too, living out their lives unaffected by or happily ignorant of the world around them. Perhaps that wasn't entirely fair—they merely chose to live out their lives without worrying about what might happen. Not like me. They didn't want to control things all the time. They didn't think all the time. They weren't interested in second guessing what was around the corner and having plans in place in order to stay ahead. Always ahead.

Manjeet had stepped up to bowl and after a short meeting between overs, Jaghtar and Vickesh had set upon a strategy—block Manjeet and hit everybody else. Manjeet approached the crease like a monsoon-powered maniac, his turban a blur of fire signalling his run-up. The growing crowd was appreciative of both the tactics employed by the batsmen and the flame-topped energy Manjeet was displaying. Stretching out his legs, Saleem looked at me and smiled.

"Quite a contest, eh? It's all nicely set up for you and me to win the game."

The rest of the team laughed at Saleem's bold claim and we applauded as Jaghtar hit another ball away smartly.

"Chota back on the roof? I assume you didn't kill him, then?"

"Nah, he sneaked up on me, the little runt, and we wrestled. It always surprises me how strong he is. I finally beat him and he produced a sack of pomegranates! That more than made up for the mango he'd eaten."

"A sack! He told me he'd only stolen one pomegranate, little liar!"

Saleem looked sideways at me and, smiling, produced another pomegranate. Wiping his knife on his trousers, he began to cut the pomegranate into little pieces.

What does that make me, then? Lying about fruit is one thing. Lying about what's happening in the real world to Bapuji is another. I'm the prince of liars. At least Chota knows when to stop. I seem to lie stronger and better as time passes until one day, I won't know the difference between truth or lies. I pulled in my knees and tried to ignore these thoughts.

After a good ten minutes of trying to disembowel Jaghtar with the ball, Manjeet threw in a slower bowl. Jaghtar swung wildly, looping the grubby white ball into the hands of a grateful Manesh. Jaghtar trudged off the dusty field but perked up at the smattering of applause he received. Fifteen minutes later, most of our team had been bowled out. Saleem was next in to bat and in preparation was cutting the air with what could pass for a cricketing stroke at a distance, but up close resembled a butcher hacking at a carcass with a cleaver. Walking on to the pitch confidently, Saleem smiled and waved to me.

"Watch you don't get your head taken off," I shouted, laughing.

"What? Not me! You just watch me, Bilal," he shouted back.

"Just take a swing at it, Saleem. Close your eyes and swing!" yelled Jaghtar.

Standing at the crease, Saleem was taking his time. Manjeet had completed his over and Rakesh was in. Saleem saw to it that everything was to his satisfaction while everyone grumbled under their breath. Finally ready, Saleem signaled for the game to continue. Just as Rakesh was about to deliver his first ball, Saleem stepped away from the crease and shook his head.

"What's the matter now?" asked Mr. Mukherjee.

"The sun's in my eyes, Masterji."

Looking up, Mr. Mukherjee sighed.

"The sun's behind you, Saleem. Get on with it, will you? We'd like to get home sometime today, perhaps even in time for dinner. Play!" And with that, Mr. Mukherjee signaled for Rakesh to bowl.

The first delivery came at Saleem fast. Unable to stop it with his bat, Saleem stuck out his backside and stopped the ball dead in its tracks. Our whole team fell about laughing as Saleem rubbed his backside. Mr. Mukherjee was smiling too. The other team was complaining that Saleem had deliberately blocked the wicket but Mr. Mukherjee ignored their pleas, gesturing for the game to continue. Saleem swung and missed the next four deliveries in quick succession. Rakesh bowled a slower delivery for his last ball. Saleem took a step forward and, planting his feet and closing his eyes, swung the bat with all his strength. The ball flew high and far over our heads straight toward the market. Cheering, we laughed as

Saleem held his bat aloft. He'd just tripled his best ever score with one shot!

But something is wrong. Skirting around the open field, I saw Mr. Mukherjee walk toward the market stall closest to us. I was a few steps behind as Mr. Mukherjee went to speak with Anand.

"Anand-ji, do you have our ball?" asked Mr. Mukherjee.

"I don't, but you'll find that son of a swine down there has it," replied Anand loudly.

"What did you call me, you dog? Say it again so we can hear it properly," replied Imtiaz angrily.

"It was loud enough the first time—or would have been if your ears weren't stuffed with dirt."

Mr. Mukherjee held up his hands and moved toward Imtiaz.

"Gentlemen, we just want our ball back. Did you see where it went?"

"Your ball nearly took out my eye, Masterji. Can't you take your kids somewhere else?" said Anand.

"If only it had taken out an eye, it might have saved you from seeing that your fruit is no good and you'd stop making a fool out of yourself," chipped in Iqbal from another stall.

Standing up, Anand moved into the small clearing. "Oh, that's big talk from behind your stale spices, Iqbal. Why don't you come out here and say it to my face like a man?"

"I would if I could see a man standing in front of me," replied Iqbal mockingly.

The tension was growing. Mr. Mukherjee, looking from one to another, held up his hands in a placating gesture.

"Please, gentlemen, there's no need for this."

Anand rounded on Mr. Mukherjee and prodded him with his finger. "Just keep your ball out of here."

"Don't blame the children—they're only playing."

"What's the matter, Anand?"

I saw the whole class slowly making their way to the marketplace. The shouting match had turned into a haranguing bout with Anand and Imtiaz in the middle shouting obscenities at each other, supported by friends and family in each corner. Mr. Mukherjee found himself right in the middle trying his best to diffuse the situation but the insults were getting worse.

"Muslims, you think you own the place . . ."

"Can you smell that? It's the smell you all give

off in this place."

"Hindus are always sticking their noses in."

"How dare you . . ."

Our class stood and watched as the argument escalated. Nudging my way to the front, I pulled at Mr. Mukherjee's sleeve.

"They're not listening, Masterji," I said quietly.

"No, they're not," he replied sadly. "Come, let's leave." He began to herd all of us away from the marketplace.

Hanging back, I grabbed Saleem by the shoulder and he looked at me curiously.

"Wait, I want to watch this," I said.

Saleem pursed his lips. "Why, Bilal?" he asked quietly.

I turned to see a group of men, their faces set in grim determination. Saleem tugged on my sleeve, making me tear my eyes away from the approaching Hindu mob.

"Bilal, look . . ." he whispered.

From our right a group of Muslims were closing fast. The groups would meet in the middle, where the argument was raging fiercely.

"Is that your brother?" asked Saleem, pointing

into the crowd.

"I don't know, I can't make anything out," I replied, straining my eyes.

Both mobs had kicked up a lot of dust and the group in the middle of the marketplace had now finally become aware of the stomping of feet. As quickly as it had formed, the crowd in the middle began to dissolve in front of our eyes and by the time the dust had settled most of the stallholders had disappeared. A few of the men still stood in the middle and, looking left and right, they picked a mob and moved toward it. Just like that. It was so easy to choose. You were one thing or another or you were a coward.

"They've got sticks, Bilal. We have to get out of here—now," Saleem hissed.

I couldn't take my eyes off the scene in front of me. A shout went up from one of the groups and in an instant the mobs closed in on each other. The dust swirled as I tried to make out what was happening. I stood watching as roughly cut bamboo sticks swung down in vicious arcs, cutting a swath through the kicked-up dirt onto an exposed skull with a sound like a thunderclap. Watching the man stagger, I took a step forward, but Saleem dragged me back. The man stumbled toward us, holding his streaming head. Seeing us, his eyes widened and he mouthed something before landing at our feet with a sickening thud, his face hitting the ground. Throwing Saleem off, I knelt down and turned the man over. We watched in horror as his body twitched a few times, his mouth contorted into a terrible shape. Finally, the man lay still. Saleem grabbed me again and lifted me to my feet. The man's eyes were open to the skies as we turned away and ran.

Chapter 17
(37 days until Partition)

"What's missing from this picture?" was one of Mr. Mukherjee's favorite questions. He would create a scenario we could all identify with that allowed us to think and provide a thoughtful response. "No guessing," he would say. "Work it out."

Sitting on my cot listening to my bapuji breathing, I wondered what was missing from my picture. Bapuji coughed loudly, a husky sound rattling his lungs. Every cough echoed around the room, bouncing off each wall and thumping my eardrums until I had to cover my ears. So much was missing. Where was our happy family? I held up a gold locket Bapuji always kept by his bedside containing a picture of my mother smiling—our sole family heirloom, aside from the books. I was only eight

116

when she died but I still remembered some things about her. How her hair always smelled of rose water and she always wore a white sari on Fridays.

When I was eight I thought that somebody dying was one big practical joke. I thought that eventually somebody would nudge me and say, "We fooled you, didn't we, Bilal? Actually, she's not gone. Keep your eye on that doorway. She'll be walking through it any minute now."

After my mother died, I remember that a lot of people came to our house to visit, sometimes bringing food, but mainly sitting in silence or praying. Saleem and I would play outside and I would often run into the quiet room only to be intercepted by Bapuji, who would gently pick me up and set me outside and stand with me for a while. It's the only time in my life I've seen Bapuji look as if he didn't want to be there, in the place that he loved so dearly. When Saleem went home each evening, I'd sit outside with an old encyclopedia looking at pictures of the jaguar or the ancient kingdoms of Rajasthan which my bapuji had once visited.

At this time, I had half an ear on the low chatter of the women who sat at the front of the house,

117

sometimes praying, and at other times cooking food for the whole street. People said it was fate that Ma was gone and that it was her time. I heard the word "fate" so many times I began to get curious. I had heard of malaria, and Saleem had once been taken with a fever so dreadful that he hadn't been able to come out and play for two whole weeks. But never before had I heard of this illness called *fate*. I resolved to find out what it was and the first place I started was the encyclopedias we had in our wall of books. After rifling through a couple of natural history encyclopedias without success, I searched the thick medical books Bapuji had collected. Still I wasn't able to find anything and I resolved to ask Doctorji about this mysterious illness. I remember Doctorji visiting to pay his respects and as he made to leave, I followed him out and tugged at his sleeve.

"What kind of illness is fate?" I asked.

He pursed his lips and bent down on one knee.

"Why do you think it's an illness, Bilal?"

I remember looking at him like he was mad and holding up my hands.

"Everybody says so. It's what Ma died of, isn't it? The thing is, I've looked through every book and can't find any mention of it anywhere and Bapuji always says that there isn't a question that can't be answered by his wall of books."

Suddenly Doctorji looked very tired and sighed. "You have the curse of curiosity, child. Like your bapuji." He put his hand on the back of my neck and pulled me close. "Bilal, fate isn't an illness, and it's not what your ma died of."

By this time, I was really confused and threw my hands in the air dramatically and blew out my cheeks.

"So why do people keep saying it was fate then?"

"Bilal, fate is a tricky subject and hard to explain. Even if I succeeded in explaining it to you, I imagine you'd find it highly unsatisfactory as an answer."

I remember pulling a face and feeling that, actually, the answer he'd just given me made no sense and was as unsatisfactory as everything else.

Doctorji looked at me, mimicking my exasperation, and shrugged his shoulders.

"You're like a gritty little dog with a knobbly bone," he muttered. "Would you like some lassi to cool off?"

Although that was a long time ago now, I remember feeling dissatisfied with what I had found out but it was a hot day and the thought of an ice-cold lassi was one I couldn't ignore.

Another racking cough made me snap out of my memories back into the present and, upon hearing Bapuji turn, I moved over to prepare his medicine. He must have heard the pestle crunching the white powder Rajahwallah had given me and he croaked at me. I took him a cool glass of water and watched him sip it slowly.

"What are you doing home? Isn't it a school day?" he asked, blinking the sleep out of his eyes.

Looking at him carefully, I took the glass from him.

"It's Saturday, Bapuji. No school for me."

Bapuji was confused and less than lucid. Just as I was preparing to give him his medicine, he sat up straight and looked at me intensely.

"Bilal, if it's Saturday we need to tend your mother's grave."

Taking the medicine over to him, I gently urged him to sit back down and made him drink the mixture.

"Bapuji, how are you going to get up there? It's treacherous getting up that path along the cliff."

Settling down a little, he grabbed my sleeve and

pulled me close.

"Well, you must go instead and tell her your news. Tell her about school and the market."

"Yes, yes, Bapuji. I'll do all that, just lie back down."

"And tell her I'm OK. I'm fine. Nothing to worry about."

"I'll do that, too, you know I will," I replied quietly.

"And tell her . . . tell her . . ."

I grabbed his arm and held it.

"I will, Bapuji. I will."

He relaxed his grip on my arm and settled back down, muttering to himself. I shuffled back to the cot and slumped down feeling heavy and lethargic. The gold locket twinkled next to me and I could see Ma smiling up at me. I'd been putting off visiting the grave for a few weeks now but Bapuji was right—I needed to tend the grave and give Ma my news.

And what news is that, Bilal? That I'm lying to Bapuji? That I've set up some elaborate scheme to keep the truth hidden? What must she think of me?

I snapped the locket shut and stood up. I needed to talk to Ma. She would understand what I was trying to do because she knew Bapuji better than anybody else. *If I leave now, I can be back before sundown,* I thought.

I made a quick note to run past Chota and let him know I was going. Gathering up some rice and a few chapatis, I made sure to take a blanket, as it became quite chilly on the cliff. As I rushed out of the door, I realized that I'd forgotten the rose water I always took with me. Sprinting back inside, I quickly grabbed the bottle and strained my ears to hear if Bapuji was still coughing but there was no sound from the other room as I ran out of the house.

Chapter 18

Every Saturday after the market had closed, we would pack some food and make our way to where Ma was buried. When she died, Bapuji was adamant that she had to be buried in a special place. At least ten different townspeople had visited Bapuji and tried to convince him that her body had to be buried, according to tradition and religion, in the cemetery just like everyone else. He had explained it all away by saying, "Well, she wasn't like everyone else."

Bapuji had recounted that, when they were younger, before I was born, he and Ma had loved to find different places to picnic and her favorite place had been the standing place of a giant banyan tree. The tree stood a few miles away from the town on a steep cliff. Bapuji had explained that the banyan tree was where the old town had originally been situated many years ago and the giant tree had been witness to all the major decisions of the village, as it was at the time. It was my great-great-grandfather who had realized the potential of the village as a central point for all the surrounding villages and convinced the elders, market traders, and village people that they needed to move, as they were slowly becoming a small town. After much discussion under the watchful eye of the banyan tree, it was decided that a move to a larger site would be made. They took everything with them but the banyan tree was immovable and had been left behind.

Bapuji and I would sit there talking to Ma as the sun went down. After a while I'd leave Bapuji to speak with her alone and I'd wander off to the other side of the tree and climb to my favorite vantage point, from which I could see the entire market town. Bapuji told me that when I was just five, I had walked around the tree, which had taken a good amount of time, and waved at Bhai, who had immediately climbed the tree and swung dangerously from a branch. I had pointed up to him and explained that that was where I wanted to be placed. Ma was totally against it but

Bapuji convinced her by saying he would climb up with me on his back.

"Hold on tight, Bilal," he'd said, and had slowly climbed up to a little kink in a branch. We sat at the top very pleased with ourselves—Bapuji because he managed to get us both up there and me because I was sitting in my bapuji's lap so high up with this great view. Ma was less pleased and I remember her standing in an emerald-colored sari at the foot of the tree, fretting and urging us all to come down. That was my first memory of us as a family, although sometimes I wondered if it was actually what I remembered or what Bapuji had told me and I had claimed as something I remembered. As I walked toward the cliff, I decided that I didn't care which it was, I was just glad I did.

Over the years, a rough path had been cut into the cliff providing a shortcut to another village a few miles east. During monsoon season, the rain often made the path treacherous. I approached the cliff, hoping it would be dry enough to attempt the climb. Looping the blanket, I tied it around my waist, and turned up the ends of my trousers. The path leading to the cliff was dry enough but as soon as I reached the beginning of the incline, I could feel the path give under my feet. Treading carefully, I'd only climbed a quarter of the way up when I felt the loose earth move under me. Suddenly I was no longer on my feet as I tumbled down the cliff amidst the rubble, mud, and shrubbery, landing with a bump.

Picking some leaves from out of my hair, I stood up and dusted myself down. The blanket was hanging too loosely around my waist so I looped it over my right shoulder and under my left armpit, tying a double knot at my chest. Clenching my teeth, I moved up the cliff once more, this time using my hands to grip firm holds, like a monkey scampering up a tree. The earth continued to slide from under me as I reached halfway up the cliff. Using every part of my body, I clung on as a loose rock threatened to sweep me back down. I stopped for a minute and, looking behind me, saw only a hazy darkness. My arms were tiring by now and, pushing up with my legs, I reached for a hold in front of me. I felt my right leg slip and I scrambled forward, clinging desperately to the cliff. I looked up just in time to see a large boulder come tumbling down toward me. Flinging myself out of its path, I lost my grip and slid down the cliff in a hail of stones and silt, racing the large boulder to the finishing line at the bottom of the cliff.

I lay on my back looking up at a colorless sky. To my side, the boulder had come to a standstill a few feet away. *So gray*, I thought, *everything looks so gray*. Picking myself up gingerly, I moved toward the boulder. Patting it with my hands, I felt the cool stone against my fingertips. The sight of the boulder made me angry and I leaned against it, my cheek tight against the stone, my shoulder pushing against its weight. But I couldn't move it. Not even an inch. Resigned, I sat with my back against the boulder and pulled my knees in.

I can't do it. Looking at the cuts on my hands and the grazes on my knees, I picked myself up and made to go back to the town. *Is that it? Give up? Is this my fate, then? To be a failure?*

Tightening the knot at my chest, I made sure the rosewater bottle was still intact and moved once more toward the path. Teeth clenched, I found holds quickly and moved up the path. Stones and debris still rattled down every time I moved but I held on to the cliff, hands curved into little hooks, legs edging inch by inch toward the top. Holding on to a piece of long grass, I pulled myself up using my feet. The rockfall had kicked up a lot of dust making it difficult to see. As I tried to blink the dust away, I looked up to see another large boulder thundering toward me—and this time there was no chance I'd be able to get out of the way in time. I watched as the boulder accelerated toward me. Closing my eyes I fixed on to an image of Bapuji in my mind. I heard a sharp sound and air whistling above my head and opened my eyes to see the boulder land behind me. It had bounced right over me! I looked for another hold and pulled myself onward.

Reaching the summit, I hauled myself over and lay on my back gasping for air. I looked over the edge and laughed, shouting at the world.

"It must be fate!"

Chapter 19

I chose a flat rock away from the giant banyan tree and sat down carefully. The elders of the town said the tree was at least two hundred years old. From this distance, the trunk resembled bands of people, shoulder to shoulder, arms entwined, standing firm together. Looking up and following each branch back then forth and into the ground, I tried to trace where the tree began and where it ended but it was impossible. It was all interconnected and growing outwards to form a massive canopy of arms spread out high above. Ma had always thought the tree was female. "Only a woman could be so beautiful and so strong," she'd said. Bapuji had smiled and agreed with her. Looking at the tree now in the dying light, I think I understood what she meant.

Once just after Ma had died, we had come out as usual on a Saturday after the market closed and Bapuji explained that the mother root would give birth to all these other roots and then plunge into the ground and out again until eventually the new roots would crowd her out.

"So what happens to the mother?" I'd asked.

"She's done her part and now has the satisfaction of watching her children grow."

"But she's invisible now."

"Not quite invisible, just hidden," Bapuji replied.

"Like Ma?"

"Yes, just like Ma."

I shook my head. *I ask some daft questions sometimes*, I thought. Wishing Bapuji was with me, I walked round the other side of the tree to where Ma was buried.

Many years ago, Bapuji had set down two flattened stones for us to sit on. I picked the one closest to the grave and laid the blanket out. Staring at the banyan tree, I began to speak.

"Ma, I've come here today to tell you that I am a liar. A deceiver. But I don't regret what I'm doing. I know that if you were here with us you would understand. I know it. You know how Bapuji is. How he can be. I know you would understand. But I still feel that somehow … I don't know … What other choice do I have now? Am I the only one who can see that everything is different? Everybody is pretending that it'll be fine. That this too shall pass. But remember you told me that a monsoon doesn't discriminate? Rich or poor, kind or cruel, we are all equal to the monsoon. And yet we carry on as normal! We go to school, market stalls open and close, we play cricket, we laugh. Meanwhile, the monsoon gathers. We are all liars, Ma. We are all great deceivers. I am a liar but I'm not the only one."

The stone underneath me felt uncomfortable so I stood up to stretch my legs and moved toward the banyan. I walked through and around the many arms of the huge tree. Spotting a little nook at the heart of the tree, I sat down in what looked like a roughly hewn seat.

"Ma, is it a just lie? Bapuji always told me that it is important to live life by your own standards and not those set by others …"

I sat at the heart of that great tree and looked out at the community of branches that had sprung up all around. Closing my eyes, I felt the rough bark of the tree with both my hands. Each root was connected to another through the soil, arms jutting toward the sky. I could sense a connection and, opening my eyes, I felt an energy moving from branch to branch.

"This is how it should be, Ma. We're all connected. There is no beginning or end."

Standing up and returning toward the grave, I saw one root that had snapped in half and hung limp. Another branch had grown on top of it and after years of growth the weight had borne down on it, bending it until it had broken. I stared at the broken branch that had ruined the symmetry of this great tree for a long while, until there were only shadows left.

I woke up suddenly. *I'm a fool, falling asleep! Bapuji is probably wondering where I am.* Rolling my shoulders, I exhaled deeply. *But I've got to relax and trust my friends—I can't always be in two places at once.*

The sun had just set as I rolled out from under my blanket and stretched. I drifted toward the edge of the cliff and saw someone waving their arms around and shouting something I couldn't hear clearly. Squinting,

I tried to make out the figure. It was Saleem! I waved back and ran to get my blanket.

Sniffing the lid of the bottle I'd brought, I sprinkled all the rose water on to the grave. I felt sad about leaving so suddenly and knelt next to the grave.

"I hope you're not angry with me, Ma. I hope you understand what I'm trying to do. I hope ..." I couldn't finish.

I ran to the cliff edge and started to make my way down carefully. Saleem waited patiently at the bottom, his arms folded. Looking me up and down, he frowned.

"What happened to you? Drag yourself through a ditch, did you?"

I looked down at myself. It was as if I'd been rolling around in the dirt.

"You wouldn't believe me if I told you, Saleem."

He smiled. "If it's got you in the story, I'd believe it. You can tell me on the way. Anyway, that's not why I'm here. Doctorji is looking for you. He came by your house and I'm sure he was a little suspicious that Manjeet, Chota, and I were loitering outside, but he didn't comment and before we could stop him he marched into your house."

133

My stomach clenched. *They must have talked. They always talk. Bapuji must know. It was all over.*

"Come on now, don't look so glum. We wanted to hear what was going on so we crept round the other side of the house to the little window and listened in but there was no sound. Your bapuji was sound asleep and Doctorji clearly didn't want to disturb him so he did a few checks and left some medicine. As he walked out of the house, he called out my name. He looked me right in the eye—you know how he does—and asked where you were. I told him you'd gone to visit your ma's grave. He said I needed to remind you that this evening you're supposed to go to the village and help him there. So here I am."

"We'd better get a move on then," I replied. "Let's go straight to Doctorji's house. He's probably getting impatient."

"I just ran all the way here, Bilal," Saleem grumbled and dragged his feet. "At least tell me why you look as if you were dragged through a ditch by an elephant."

"OK, OK, but get a move on," I said. "You know how slippery that cliff is after the rains? Well, let me tell you . . ."

Chapter 20

Doctorji lived in a small house on the outskirts of town, away from the market. He always seemed apart from everyone, keeping a certain distance between himself and the people he served. I asked him about it once.

"Doctorji, why do you stay away from everyone else? Do you not like living with people?"

As usual, he'd looked right at me and considered his answer. Doctorji was not one for rushing.

"I serve the people most importantly in two ways. One, I look after their physical health and two, I act as a justice. As a justice, I must always be fair and objective. You know these words, Bilal?"

"No, I don't," I replied.

"They mean that I must always distance myself

from the situation over which I'm presiding. If there's a dispute or problem where I have to decide on a just action and we happen to be close friends I must not let that bias my decision. Does that make sense?"

"Yes, I think so, Doctorji. Friends are a nuisance you just don't need."

I remember that Doctorji had smiled then. He smiled so little that I could easily count all the instances when I'd made him smile, usually with some silly comment.

Now Saleem and I stood outside Doctorji's door and knocked. After a few minutes, Doctorji appeared with his medical bag. Looking at my bedraggled state, he tutted and pursed his lips.

"Well, I'm ready to go but clearly you're not," he said, picking a twig from my hair.

Saleem snorted but stopped when Doctorji glared at him. I shuffled from foot to foot and grimaced.

"It was quite difficult climbing that cliff. The rains have made it treacherous," I said.

"I see. So you thought it would be a good idea to climb it? Honestly, Bilal, you could have broken your neck or been squashed to a pulp by a falling boulder. Well, go home and get cleaned up. I went to see your bapuji today and he was sleeping restfully. He won't need more medicine for a couple of days."

"But, Doctorji, I think I should stay here. In case he needs me."

"I think you could do with a break, Bilal. A little time away will give you some perspective."

"But, Doctorji—"

"I need your help, Bilal."

"Yes, but I'm not sure . . ."

"I'd like it if you could accompany me tomorrow," said Doctorji firmly. "I take it Saleem is able to look in on your bapuji and make sure he takes the right amount of medicine while you're away with me?"

"I'll make sure he takes it, Doctorji," replied Saleem promptly.

"Good. Now off you go, Bilal. Go and get some rest. I'll see you back here tomorrow morning. Go on now."

Grabbing Saleem, I started walking quickly toward town.

"What are we going to do now? Maybe I should pretend that I'm not well."

Saleem looked at me sideways and shook his head.

"You know Doctorji can sniff out a liar at a hundred

paces." Realizing what he'd said, Saleem smiled. "Well, maybe not all the time but you know what I mean. It's not worth the risk, he'll only get suspicious."

"Yes, but I'll be too far away from here."

"We said we'd help you so let us. Go with Doctorji and leave the rest to us. I'll make sure nobody gets in to see your bapuji, OK?"

As we approached the house we joined Chota, who was loitering outside. I put my arms around Saleem and Chota.

"OK, but if anything happens, send me a message via pigeon. Ask Manjeet to ask his cousin to send one and I'll come right home."

Chapter 21

I had been accompanying Doctorji to the villages surrounding our market town for the last two years. Bapuji used to go with Doctorji for many years but then the market had kept him too busy so he began to send me instead. We would choose a book of stories together and I'd take it with me to read to the village children. For years they had enjoyed it when Bapuji told the stories so when I turned up one day, book in hand, they had taken some convincing. After a few pointers from Bapuji, I managed to work out what the children liked and since then they looked as if they actually enjoyed it when I arrived. The stories weren't the main reason why we went to the village. Once a month, Doctorji would gather up whatever medicine he could spare, along with a number of other things the village people had ordered from some of the market vendors, and load it up on his donkey cart. The villagers would come to Doctorji with their complaints and, assisted by me, he would try his best to treat the various ailments.

The sun was high in the sky when we left town. I sat next to Doctorji as the donkey pulled us along in the small cart. Rocking in the rhythm of the jostling cart, I made myself comfortable. The surrounding land was flat and stretched out in front of us in a sea of green and brown. After the hustle of the market town, the silence was complete with only the snorting of the donkey and the creaky turning of the wheels clipping it. The sky pulsed blue and white above our heads, and the threat of monsoon seemed far away.

As Doctorji stopped the cart to speak with a woman who had flagged him down to ask about a complaint her husband was suffering from, I closed my eyes and let the silence calm me. We moved through the countryside waving at people and stopping occasionally to speak with farmers and old women who recognised Doctorji. Many people invited us in to have some tea or food but Doctorji declined as politely as he could and promised he'd try to visit soon. We slowly made our way across the land and I felt a sense of well-being enveloping me like a blanket.

"It's so quiet here. So peaceful," I whispered to myself.

Doctorji looked at me and, nodding his assent, went back to staring off into the distance. From the corner of my eye, I glanced at him to see if he would say something but he had settled into a rhythm with his cart.

"It can't always be like this, can it, Doctorji?"

Doctorji sighed and shook his head. "Son, the peace has already been disturbed," he said.

"Broken," I replied absently.

"What?" said Doctorji, nonplussed.

"The peace has been broken. Some things can't be fixed if they are broken," I replied.

"No, you're right, but they can be mended or they can heal over a period of time."

"How long is a period of time?" I asked.

"That depends on the will of the person, Bilal."

"What if the will isn't there, Doctorji?"

"Then even though the body heals, the mind will

never allow you to fully heal."

"It's always about will, isn't it, Doctorji?" I said, staring at the path stretching ahead of us.

"It's an important part, Bilal. Take your bapuji as an example. Despite everything, his will is strong. His body has failed him but his mind still props him up," said Doctorji. "His will cannot be extinguished."

"No, it can't."

"You're more like him than you realize, Bilal. You have his need to see and to know and understand. Like him, you're like a sponge absorbing everything life has to offer," said Doctorji, glancing at me.

"Sometimes I'd rather not be like that."

"Yes, I can see how that constant need to find the meaning in things could be wearing," said Doctorji, smiling.

"You're not like that, Doctorji," I said.

"No, logic is my best friend. I believe in cause and effect, my boy. One thing happens because of another. There is no greater meaning, there is only what you do and what happens as a consequence."

"That's what I want to believe! That's how I want to live my life," I said defiantly. Doctorji looked at me curiously and pursed his lips.

"You are your bapuji's son, Bilal."

"But it's not realistic, Doctorji," I whispered, hating the fact that I appeared to be betraying my bapuji.

"What isn't realistic?"

"To believe life will always work itself out. That whatever will be, will be, and it's best not to worry and to just let things happen," I replied.

"But if that's what you believe, Bilal, if that's your character ..."

"If it is, then it's best to change. I don't want to be a dreamer all my life. I'd rather live in the real world with everyone else," I said, hardly daring to look at him.

"Sometimes, Bilal, the real world is ugly," replied Doctorji.

"Maybe, but at least it's real," I said.

Chapter 22

Entering the village, we were approached by children who ran alongside the cart. I waved the thick, heavy book I'd chosen to read at them and they cheered in anticipation. Beaming at their enthusiasm, I jumped off the cart, surrounded by children. Doctorji pulled into his usual place in front of a disused hut. As he went off to meet with the village leaders, I was inundated with questions about the "big town" but eventually I managed to extract myself and went to look for Doctorji. I found him standing near a gathering of men. Walking over, I could sense a tenseness in the way he stood and out of the corner of my eye I could see that there was a heated debate going on, with a few looks being sent Doctorji's way.

"Doctorji, is something the matter?"

Doctorji hadn't realized I was standing next to him and he quickly shook his head. *Too quickly.*

"No, no, everything's fine. They're just discussing where they want us to start."

That's a lie, I thought. Watching the agitated group, it was clear that there were two sides. One for and one against. *Against what?*

I could sense Doctorji becoming more anxious. His whole body was still and although he looked as if he was admiring the blue sky, his attention was solely on the conversation going on not ten yards from us.

Finally, the group came to some kind of resolution and a short, elderly man signaled to Doctorji that he could begin his work. I moved toward the cart to unload some of the medicine we'd brought with us.

While unloading the cart, Doctorji leaned in close and whispered in my ear, "Something's not right. I'm not sure what's happened but as soon as we're finished, we're leaving. Assemble the children and begin your story now. It might provide us with a little goodwill just in case."

"In case of what?" I asked, alarmed.

"Just in case," was all that Doctorji would say and

he strode off to the crowd of people who were waiting impatiently.

Anxiously, I walked toward the groups of children and asked them to gather around a clearing near the well at the edge of the village. There was a good crowd of mostly younger children sitting patiently in front of me in the bright afternoon light. The men of the village were still gathered together and were talking less animatedly but still sending wary glances from time to time toward Doctorji. Making myself as comfortable as possible, I looked at the eager faces and cleared my throat.

"Today, I thought I'd read you the story of Aladdin and his magic lamp . . ."

Upon finishing the story, some of the young ones cheered and asked for another, but just then two men strode to where I was sitting and stopped in front of me.

"Come with us," they said quietly.

"Where to?" I asked, nervous at their rigid stance and the look in their eyes.

"Just come. Doctorji is waiting for you. Come."

I picked up my book but they signaled for me to leave it. A little girl—who always sat in the front row of any story I told—stood up and took the book from me.

"I'll look after it for you. You can have it back later," she said and held the book close to her chest.

Smiling, I nodded at her, muttered thanks, and stepped into line with the two men away from the silent ring of children.

We approached the disused hut where we had left our cart and stopped outside. They signaled for me to enter. I walked in and heard the door shut behind me followed by the thud of a heavy wooden bar being put into place. Doctorji sat in the corner on a sack of rice. His face was still but I could see thunderclouds in his eyes and something else—fear.

"Doctorji, what's going on?"

Doctorji stood up and began pacing the room. He approached the door and listened. Satisfied there was no one on the other side, he sat back down.

"Bilal, this is what we spoke of. The peace has been broken and we are far from home. After completing my duties and distributing the medicine, the village elders—well, mostly young men from what I could see—marched me here. They asked if I was a spy sent by the Muslims to count their number and take vital information back to the massing hordes who are waiting to attack."

Finally, the danger of the situation hit me and I sat down opposite Doctorji with my head in my hands.

"Why would they think that? I mean, we've been coming here for years. You've been coming here even longer than me. How could they think that?"

Doctorji stood up and began pacing again.

"There have been riots and looting in many places. A relative of one of the villagers arrived at the same time we did and told all the village elders some of the stories of violence around the country. Most of the people here aren't convinced by them and spoke out but the young men seem to hold sway here. Fueled by the relative's terrible stories, they managed to convince everybody that it was in the interests of the village to hold us."

Doctorji looked straight at me and stopped pacing, aware that it was making me nervous watching him prowl back and forth.

"But what are they going to do with us now? We're not spies. When are they going to let us go? I have to get back to Bapuji!" I cried. Panicking, my stomach cramped, making me bend over in pain. Doctorji came to my side.

"Stomach cramps again? We have to stay calm, Bilal. This is probably all just talk. Once the villagers realize that they're overreacting, we can get back home. Relax your stomach and stop clenching your teeth. Take a deep breath and let your body relax. We'll be fine, we just have to be patient."

Leaning back, I tried to breathe slowly. What could they possibly do to us? We hadn't done anything wrong. We were trying to help by bringing people medicine. I shut my eyes. *We just have to be patient. But what are we waiting for?*

Chapter 23

The hours crawled by as I watched Doctorji pace around the hut. Many years ago, the market town committee had decided to set up a scheme to aid the local villages by providing them with better medicine. Doctorji had volunteered to administer to the villagers and take what little medicine the market town was able to spare. In all that time, we had always been treated with the utmost respect. Often the villagers would ask us to stay another day because they seldom had visitors. I laughed out loud at the thought of these gentle villagers, who always thought of Doctorji's more modern methods and medicine as strange, wanting to kill us. I noticed Doctorji had stopped pacing and was staring at me, clearly startled at my laughter.

"What's so funny?" Doctorji asked.

"The thought of these villagers trying to do us harm. It just doesn't make sense. What could they possibly do to us?"

It was getting dark now. The little barred window let in a beam of moonlight outlining the tracks Doctorji's pacing had created on the floor. It was a strange and beautiful pattern in a figure of eight. I chuckled again. *Typical*, I thought. It was just like Doctorji to pace nervously but still maintain a well-ordered pattern. I went to the window and looked out. The moonlight had bathed everything in a silver light and shadows jumped at every turn.

"It's not worth thinking about what they could do to us, Bilal. These are strange times. Difficult times. People aren't behaving how they normally would so we can't depend on them to behave rationally."

Doctorji began pacing again as I tried to make sense of what he had said. I stood up and began to pace in the opposite direction.

As the night wore on, I thought of all the terrible things the villagers could do to us. The many ways in which they could harm or kill us. My pacing intensified until I caught up with Doctorji and almost

151

clipped his ankles. Putting his hands on my shoulders, he held me firmly. As we locked eyes, I noticed for the first time the deep lines around his eyes, like little incisions made with a scalpel.

With a grating sound, we suddenly heard the bar being lifted. We froze. Doctorji motioned for me to sit down away from the door and stood in the middle of the room, hands on hips. Two young men walked in with scarves wrapped around their faces. They stopped, whispered something to one another, then advanced.

"Now look," said Doctorji, "I've been coming here for eight years and never have I been treated in this—"

Without warning, the larger of the men slapped Doctorji hard in the face while the other one punched him in the stomach.

"Shut your mouth, you dog! How stupid do you think we are?"

Stunned, it took me a minute to realize what was going on. I watched in horror as the shorter man produced a stick and raised it high in the air. Yelling, I jumped at him and, taking him by surprise, we both went down in a heap. After the initial surprise, the man recovered and pinned my arms.

"Look, boy, if you don't shut up, I'm going to take this stick to your head. Understand?"

Reluctantly, I stopped struggling. Moving off me slowly and pointing the stick at me, he nodded at the other man.

"We just want to ask some questions. After that we'll let you go."

Doctorji was now sitting up but still looked winded. Sucking in deep breaths of air, he held up his hand and agreed. "Ask your questions," he wheezed.

"Who sent you?" asked the larger man.

"I told you, we were sent by the market town committee. Like always."

The two men looked at each other, puzzled, and shrugged.

"Have the Muslims overrun your town? Is that what you're trying to tell us?" demanded the smaller man.

"No, of course not," said Doctorji. "What I'm saying is that—"

The smaller man swung the stick in a vicious arc and connected with Doctorji's nose. I threw myself at him again, grabbing hold of his stick, but he was ready for me this time and, holding my neck with his free hand, he threw me to the ground. The bigger man moved toward me and pinned me against the floor.

"We know you're a doctor—some of the villagers here even think you're a good man—but you don't fool me. Just tell us how many people there are waiting to attack us so that we can make the necessary arrangements. You'd be saving a lot of bloodshed. Think of that."

His nose streaming with blood, Doctorji sat upright and tilted his head back.

"Does it matter what I say, boy? You've already made up your mind about why we're here. I've been coming here for eight years to provide medicine and aid for the people of the village. But I've never seen you here before, either of you. What are you? Political agitators?"

"You don't have to worry about who we are."

"No, you're right, I don't. Because in six months or a year or however long it takes, I'll come back here. The villagers will look at me with guilt but you won't be here, will you? You'll be gone, feeding off the next frenzy in the next town."

"You don't know what you're saying, old man. The villagers asked us to come. We're here to help them find out the truth."

Bringing his head down and staring at both men, Doctorji smiled, the blood streaming down his nose coloring his mouth and teeth, making him look frightening in the moonlight.

"Son, my donkey knows more about the truth than you do."

The men looked at one another and then advanced on Doctorji. The big man also produced a stick and both began to pound him as he curled up into a little ball. Shouting for help, I jumped on the big man's back but he lifted me off and hit me hard in the face, the force of it flinging me on to the floor. I tried to stand up but the smaller man kicked me in the stomach. Helpless, I watched as Doctorji took the beating without a sound. It was only after they'd stopped that I realized I'd been screaming enough for both of us.

Stepping over me, they pulled open the heavy door and turned round.

"Look, we tried to help you by giving you a chance but there are others who'll be here in the morning who aren't so forgiving."

Holding my stomach, I watched as they left, slamming the door shut and replacing the bar across it. Doctorji had dragged himself upright. I crawled over to him on all fours and leaned heavily against a sack of rice.

"Are you all right, Doctorji?"

"No broken bones. I think that was just the warm-up act, though—the real thugs will be here by morning," said Doctorji, slowly moving the tip of his nose and wincing.

"Can't you just lie to me?" I asked.

"Lie? About what?" he replied incredulously.

"About what could happen. Tell me everything will be OK."

"What's the point of that?"

"It would make me feel better," I said quietly.

"Only for a while, until you realize the truth," Doctorji said grimly.

"But by then it wouldn't matter."

"It would matter to me," said Doctorji, grimacing in pain as he tried to sit comfortably. "There are a few more hours until dawn. It's no use worrying now. Let's sit and see what comes."

Staring at the smudged figure of eight on the dusty floor, my legs felt like they were still moving. A thousand thoughts tried to break free from my head.

I have to get home. I need to be near Bapuji. Desperation crept into my mind and the sight of Doctorji sitting opposite me with his shoulders slumped, holding his head in his hands, was almost too much to bear.

"Doctorji?"

"Yes, Bilal," replied Doctorji without looking up.

"I need to tell you something ... about what I've been doing recently ..."

*

After I'd told Doctorji about the lie, I didn't feel better or worse. His face stayed passive but I knew he was weighing up what I'd said.

Doctorji didn't have time to tell me what he thought because there was a scratching sound at the door. I closed my eyes and listened carefully in case my ears were playing tricks on me. There it was again! But Doctorji hadn't stirred from his thoughtful pose. I quickly moved toward the door and put my ear to it. Doctorji noticed and stood up.

"What is it?" he asked.

"I heard a scratching at the door. I think there's somebody on the other side."

We both put our ears against the door and listened. The scratching sound continued.

"Hello? Can you hear me?" I whispered.

"Hello," a little voice whispered from the other side.

"Hello! Can you tell us what's happening? What are they going to do to us?"

More silence. I could hear Doctorji's heartbeat drumming steadily next to me.

"They think you're spies. They think that if you're allowed to leave you'll go and tell whoever it is to attack us and steal all our women. They think . . . "

This time the silence was deafening. Now I could hear my own heartbeat thumping inside my chest.

"They think what?" I whispered.

"They think it best if you're not allowed to leave."

"Do you think you can help us?" Doctorji asked quietly.

"How can I help you?" the voice whispered.

"Can you open this door and let us out?"

There was a shuffling sound outside which stopped suddenly.

Please, don't leave us here.

"I'm not tall enough to reach the bar. It's just out of my reach."

"There must be something you can stand on—a

barrel or something?"

"It's all too heavy for me to move," said the voice.

"And it would make too much noise anyway," I added.

"There *must* be something you can use," said Doctorji. Sensing desperation in his voice, I leaned close to the door.

"It's OK, take your time. We're not going anywhere," I tried to joke.

Nobody laughed. The light in the hut was changing and dawn was not far away. If we didn't escape now we might never leave. As we pressed our ears to the door, we heard some more shuffling and then little footsteps running away. I looked at Doctorji in horror at the realization that we were alone again. He stepped away and, setting his jaw, walked slowly back to his sack of rice. I turned my back on the door and slid down to the floor, head resting in my hands. We were far from home and surrounded by strangers. This was not how I'd thought it would be. I had only ever known the market town. It was where I thought I would live and die. I had been so sure of it that the possibility of anything else was like a slap across my face.

Abruptly, I heard returning footsteps and more shuffling outside the door. Grunting sounds followed and, with a grinding noise that sounded as if it would wake the whole village, the bar was lifted from its resting place. The door was slowly nudged open and there before us was the little girl, standing on the thick, heavy book I'd given her. Smiling, she stepped off the book and very carefully picked it up, blowing the dust off its surface. Doctorji was at my side looking curiously at the girl with my book, then he quickly went to our donkey cart.

"Why did you come for us?" I asked.

"I wanted to give your book back to you like I said I would."

Doctorji returned hurriedly. "We have to go now, before the village wakes." He smiled at the girl and went back to the cart.

Kneeling down, I grinned at her. "We have to leave now. Thank you so much for your help."

"That's OK. I didn't want them to hurt you," she replied.

"Thanks to you they won't. But you mustn't tell anybody about this and you must go back home and pretend this never happened."

"OK." And she held the book out in front of me.

"No, this book is now yours. I give it to you for your help. Just tell them that I forgot it or something. I hope it brings you great pleasure."

The little girl's eyes widened in surprise and she held the book close to her chest. I kissed her forehead and ran to the cart. Waving good-bye, we quickly made our way out of the village.

Chapter 24

We approached the town weary and stiff from the ride and a weight settled on me as soon as we entered it. My limbs felt like lead and my head drooped to my chest. But I lifted my head. I was home and Bapuji needed me. It was no time to feel weak. Doctorji sat upright as ever and led the cart straight to his house. Stepping off the cart, he grimaced slightly at the stiffness or pain he must have felt.

"Bilal, we mustn't tell anyone about this. Certain members of the committee might use this to tip things over the edge. Leave it with me. If we don't say anything, technically we're not lying."

Looking at Doctorji's haggard face, I nodded. *So it's not technically a lie until you open your mouth. Right. It seems the rules of lying are more subtle than I thought.*

"I'll keep it to myself." *I can do that.*

"Check on your bapuji and see if he's OK. I visited him before we left and the medicine seemed to be giving him some relief. Make sure he drinks a lot of water and give him some fresh fruit. I'll come to check on him soon."

"Yes, Doctorji. I'll see you later."

Jumping off the cart, I made to move past Doctorji but he stopped me and squeezed my shoulder.

"About the other thing . . . about your bapuji . . ." he started.

The weight of my confession hit me squarely between my shoulders, almost bearing me down to the ground.

"We need to talk about that, too," Doctorji said quietly and turned away.

Chapter 25

I trudged my way into town then went to our vantage point and hailed Chota. His head appeared at the top of the old house and he waved me up.

"What's the news, Chota? Where's Saleem?" I asked.

"I'm not sure where he is—some problem at home, I think."

"What kind of problem?"

"He didn't say but he promised he'd be back shortly. Oh, and he said to tell you that your bapuji woke up yesterday and wondered where you were. He also asked Saleem if there were any newspapers around as he wanted to catch up with what was going on. Saleem made some excuse and left but your bapuji asked him to get a paper by tomorrow."

"He can't read a newspaper! He'll know in an instant what's going on! All the papers have news about the partition plan and it will break his heart." *I knew that he'd want to see a newspaper eventually.*

"But he wanted to read one and you know what he's like when he gets an idea in his head," Chota replied, shrugging his shoulders. "He's a bit like you. Once the idea's there, there's no getting rid of it."

I rubbed my eyes and sighed deeply. Chota was shaking his head.

"What are you looking at me like that for?" I asked.

"What are you looking so miserable for?" Chota replied. "Just think it through. There is always an answer if you think hard enough."

I rubbed my forehead. *Chota always thinks everything is so simple!* But I thought it best to humor him.

"And what's that then?" I asked tiredly.

"Well, you'll just have to print your own newspaper, won't you? Simple."

Chota went back to paring a piece of wood, entirely satisfied with himself. I closed my eyes in irritation. Suddenly, it hit me. Chota *was* right! I needed to print my own paper with my own version of events. I patted Chota on the back, thanked him, and said good-bye.

I arrived home in time for the midday meal. Bapuji was dozing when I returned and I set about cooking rice and making some daal to eat with it. As the rice was cooking, I sat down on the bed at Bapuji's feet. He was breathing evenly and coughing less but he was still so thin; apart from his head propped up against a pillow, it would be difficult to tell if there was anybody under the thick blanket. Bapuji had always been slight but his skin now hung off him, stretched taut over his frame as if somebody had laced him up too tight from behind, like toughened, tan leather shoes. His cheeks had sunken inwards, as had his eyes, so that when he looked at you, only two shiny glints appeared, like two lone stars in a dark sky.

I began to gently massage his legs, waking them back to life.

"Wake up, Bapuji," I said quietly.

Bapuji opened his eyes with a smile as if waking from a distant dream.

"Ah, you're back. It felt like you were gone for weeks. How was it?" he asked.

"Oh, you know, the usual. We did our bit, they did theirs," I replied as calmly as I could.

That answer seemed to satisfy Bapuji and he slowly

tried to sit up.

"We're going to have lunch," I said, and brought the rice and daal through.

"I'm not very hungry," Bapuji sighed.

"You have to eat. You can't do all that dreaming and not eat," I replied.

"That's true, dreaming is a tiring business. Who knows how long you travel for when you're dreaming —maybe days, years, centuries, even."

Grabbing my stool, I handed Bapuji his plate and sat down with my own. I was hungry and set about eating heartily.

"The funny thing about dreaming is how real it all seems sometimes," Bapuji continued. "You can almost taste it and then you wake up and it slips through your fingers like a handful of soil before you can hold on to it and mould it into shape. The only dreams I remember are about you and your ma."

Still wolfing down my food, I nodded my head. Bapuji hadn't started his yet. I pointed to his plate and made a face. He held up his hand in submission and began to eat.

"Maybe they're not dreams that you have about Ma and me. Maybe they're imaginings or just

167

memories," I said.

"Hmm, that's an interesting way of looking at it. What do you dream about, Bilal?"

"*About you not dying, Bapuji,*" I wanted to say. "*About Ma still being here with us.*"

"I don't dream much, Bapuji. I daydream a lot, though," I replied.

"About what?"

"Oh, you know, being better at cricket, soaring through the sky like an eagle, organizing the market town, things like that."

"All good dreams, dear heart," said Bapuji. Looking down at his plate, he held up his hand again. "I think this is all I can manage, my boy. Please don't be angry with me—I don't seem to have much of an appetite nowadays."

The food had barely been touched but merely moved around the plate. I took it from him.

"OK, but Doctorji said that I should feed you fresh fruit, so I brought you a pomegranate. It's a ripe one. You can cut it in your special way for both of us to eat."

Bapuji took the pomegranate and small knife from me. He held the pomegranate in the palm of his hand

and slipped the knife in at an angle. He proceeded to make cuts right the way around. Just before he made the final cut he looked at me and smiled. Making a little circular cut at the top, he removed the knife and the fruit opened up like a flower. Red stones glistened like little rubies in the palm of his hand.

Chapter 26

Morning sunlight filtered through the cracks of our home and flecked the room with little spots of yellow. Opening one sleep-filled eye, I noticed how the shafts of light peppered the wall of books and I propped myself up on one elbow to see which books had attracted the sunrays. Despite the sun there was a chill in the room.

Hearing Bapuji stir, I went to make some tea. As I was stirring the pot, Saleem came bounding through the door and squatted down next to me.

"Tea for three?" he asked.

"No choice now that you're here breathing hot air down my neck!" I said and nudged Saleem, throwing him off balance and sending him sprawling. Growing serious, he sat up and looked at me as I poured the tea into cups.

"Bilal, my bapuji said something to us all the other day. Something about—"

"Bilal," croaked Bapuji from the other room.

Leaving Saleem to sip his tea, I grabbed the blanket from my bed and covered Bapuji, pulling it up to his neck. He woke suddenly and smiled at seeing me.

"I was still dreaming," he said.

"You're always dreaming, Bapuji," I replied, chuckling.

"Not always—nowadays I sleep more than anything."

Propping him up on a pillow, I handed Bapuji his steaming hot tea. A shaft of sunlight filtered through the bamboo outside the window and bathed his face. Under that bright light, his skin looked translucent and I could make out the veins under his skin. I tried to look away but couldn't take my eyes from the paper-thin skin, sunken eyes, and wispy hair. In that half light there was more of a resemblance to a human skull than a human head. I watched as Bapuji leaned into the light, letting the warmth bathe his face. Watching him bask in the sunlight reminded me of a flower leaning into the sun to catch its most potent rays. It was nature's way, Mr. Mukherjee said. To bloom, to live. Taking the cup from him, I kissed Bapuji on his forehead and helped him settle down into the bed. His eyes already looked heavy again. As I turned to go, he clasped my hand gently.

"Bilal, I feel like I'm slipping away," he said quietly.

"Don't say that, Bapuji. You're still here," I replied.

Squeezing my hand, he nodded. "You're right, I am. But I'd still like to be a part of the world in some way. You haven't brought me a newspaper in a while, Bilal. News of the outside world would perk me up, I'm sure. Bring me a newspaper, will you?"

"Of course but the problem is, er . . . that there's a strike on at the moment. You might have to wait a little while for the news."

"Strange. It must be a serious strike for the newspapers not to be delivered. Still, it'll be over soon, surely?"

"By next week it should all be over and I'll get a paper for you. Now rest and I'll check on you later."

"OK, Bilal, OK," he replied, closing his eyes and holding the blanket close to his chest.

I walked back into the other room, where Saleem was still squatting and sipping his tea.

"Did you hear that?" I asked.

He nodded and took a deep gulp of his tea. "Yes. What do you have in mind?"

"We need to go to see Mr. Singh and convince him to print a paper for us," I replied.

"Just like that, ask him to print it?" Saleem asked.

"Yes, just like that." And with that I marched off with Saleem following behind me.

Chapter 27
(26 days until Partition)

On the other side of the market, behind the spice section, stood Mr. Singh's printer's yard. We walked quickly through the market and I noticed that some of the stalls were eerily empty. Approaching the yard, I tried to dredge up what I remembered about Mr. Singh but couldn't really think of anything useful apart from that he was about the same age as Bapuji. I vaguely remembered Bapuji visiting him when he needed something printed for the committee. Standing in front of his door, I tried to think of the best way to tackle this.

"What are you going to say?" asked Saleem.

"I'm not sure but play along, will you?" I said, knocking on the door.

Mr. Singh didn't look the slightest bit happy to see two boys standing outside his door. He looked down at us, his bearded face wearing a scowl.

"What do you want?" he growled.

"Hello, Mr. Singh. We're here because we need your help please," I said.

"Help with what?" The frown deepened.

"Well, we're doing a school project and one of the tasks is to create a special newspaper. Most of the class is going to handwrite their newspapers but we thought it would be good if we could get ours printed. We really want to make an impression, don't we, Saleem?"

Saleem looked at me with bug-like eyes and nodded slowly. I nodded back at him and slapped him on his shoulder.

"I wish I could claim the idea as my own but it was Saleem here who thought it up," I said cheerfully.

Mr. Singh turned his attention to Saleem and scowled, clearly blaming him for disturbing him that particular day. Saleem busily inspected a pebble with his toe. Mr. Singh still had his hand on the door and blocked the entire doorway with his considerable bulk. He gently swung the door back and forth as if he hadn't quite decided what he wanted to do.

"So Mr. Mukherjee sent you?" he asked, narrowing his eyes.

Saleem was really bothering the pebble now and was visibly wilting under the glare of Mr. Singh's attention.

"No, no, no, absolutely not. We can't tell Mr. Mukherjee for two reasons. One, we want it to be a surprise so that he's impressed with our initiative. And two, we don't want anyone in the class to find out or else they'll all be here knocking on your door, bothering you and asking you all sorts of dumb things. We don't want that now, do we, Mr. Singh?" I asked confidently.

"No, we really don't," replied Mr. Singh and, sighing, he opened the door to let us in. "You'd better come in then, but don't touch anything or sit on anything or ask any dumb questions."

"No, Mr. Singh, we won't," I replied, grabbing Saleem by the arm and pulling him into the house.

Mr. Singh disappeared into another room and left Saleem and I to grin at each other for having made it this far. When Mr. Singh returned he sat down on a stool. It looked like it had seen better days and supporting Mr. Singh's bulk couldn't have helped.

"Now, where's the text I'll be printing? Let me warn you, I won't write or edit it for you. You have to prepare your own text and have it ready for printing. Also, I can only print you a front cover, two inside pages, and a back page. That's my maximum for this kind of thing and even that's being generous, let me tell you."

Looking over at Saleem, I smiled. "Of course. We're just in the process of putting the text together. It'll be ready in the next few days. We want it to be perfect. I'm sure you understand, Mr. Singh."

Growling and shifting on his rickety stool, Mr. Singh waved his hands impatiently. "Just have it here by Friday or else I might change my mind."

"Friday is exactly when we were thinking of, wasn't it, Saleem? We'll get it to you before then, no problem."

"See that you do. Now don't you have to go to school or something? Go on, off you run or you'll be late." And with that he ushered us out and slammed the door shut behind us.

I beamed at Saleem. He put his arm around me and started walking me in the direction of the school.

"Now there's just the small matter of writing the thing! And what happens when Mr. Singh reads it?"

asked Saleem.

"One day at a time, Saleem, that's all I can do at the moment," I replied.

Saleem nodded his head and we dashed through the strangely empty streets.

Chapter 28

Arriving late at school, we hid behind the door waiting for the moment when Mr. Mukherjee would turn his back and write on the blackboard. Manjeet, who was sitting at the back, saw us and made two spaces for us either side of him. Timing it just right, we tiptoed into the classroom just as Mr. Mukherjee had turned to highlight something on the board. Sitting down quickly, we attentively stared at the board, looking as if we were absorbed with what he was saying. I settled down to the comforting sound of Mr. Mukherjee's voice, all the while thinking about how I would put the newspaper together.

What will I write? I've never written so much in my life.

*

As the day wore on, I became more agitated at the thought of what I'd undertaken.

Write a newspaper? What was I thinking? And what if Mr. Singh tells somebody? Or what if he decides to ask Mr. Mukherjee about the "school project"? What if he comes to the house to see Bapuji?

When you tell the truth, nobody bats an eyelid. When you lie, still nobody bats an eyelid. The only difference is how you feel. The worse you feel when you lie, the more problems you'll have. I decided not to feel bad about anything.

A sharp dig in my ribs interrupted my thoughts. The school day was over and Mr. Mukherjee was finishing up.

"I'll see you tomorrow and don't forget your books. Everyone can go except Bilal and Saleem—I'd like a quick word with you two."

Shuffling our feet, we waited for the class to empty and went to stand at Mr. Mukherjee's desk. He continued to gather his papers and files while we stood there trying not to look at each other. Saleem was doing a little dance from one foot to the other and scrunching up his face. Finally, Mr. Mukherjee looked up.

"So, why were you so late this morning? The school day starts at the same time every morning. You both live five minutes' walk from the school. There are boys here that come from the neighboring village and they're always on time. So tell me, what's your excuse?"

Saleem was still jiggling about and didn't look as if he was capable of saying anything so I cleared my throat.

"Well, Masterji, erm ... Saleem came to my house so we could go to school together. I made some tea for Bapuji and just as we were about to leave, I realized that I'd forgotten to mix his medicine so I had to do that quickly. Saleem said he would wait for me and so we were both late coming in." *It's getting easier and easier to lie.*

Mr. Mukherjee looked right at us then stood up and checked his pocket watch.

"That doesn't explain why one minute you weren't in my class and the next you'd magically appeared. Why didn't you just wait at the door and explain that when you arrived rather than sneaking in?"

"We didn't want to disturb your lesson, Masterji. We just thought ..."

"No, you're lying. And what is the matter with you, Saleem? Why are you pulling such faces at me?"

"Masterji, sir, I really need to go to the toilet."

"Off you go then. I don't want a puddle in my classroom, not after the flood we had with Amit last time. Go on."

Saleem walked out of the classroom on tiptoes being careful not to make any sudden movements.

Mr. Mukherjee removed his glasses and rubbed his eyes.

"What's going on with you, Bilal?"

"Nothing, Masterji, nothing is going on with me," I replied, shrugging my shoulders.

"I know it's a difficult time for you with your bapuji . . . but you still need to . . . let these things out. You can't keep your feelings bottled up or else one day you'll explode."

Better to keep them bottled up than let them out, I thought. *Who would understand them?*

Mr. Mukherjee sighed and sat me down. Putting his hand on my shoulder, he squeezed gently.

"Is there anything you would like to tell me?"

"There's nothing to tell, I—I . . ." Stuttering, I tried to shrug off Mr. Mukherjee's hand but he held firm.

"Tell me, please," he asked.

"I don't know what you mean, Masterji, really . . . I, er . . . There's nothing," I replied, feeling tired all of a sudden. Mr. Mukherjee's hand felt as heavy as a sack of potatoes.

Saleem came back into the room and stood by my side. He put his arm on my other shoulder.

"Tell him, Bilal," he said quietly.

Stung, I looked up at him. *Don't betray me!*

"You can't take it all on your shoulders all the time, Bilal. I can help you but so can others. Tell Masterji."

What is he saying? Shaking my head, I was inundated with thoughts, memories, ideas, lies, plans, dreams . . . I doubled over feeling my insides crunch with pain. Mr. Mukherjee knelt down next to me and spoke to me gently while Saleem looked on worriedly.

"Breathe, Bilal, and relax. Your stomach has a knot in it and you need to relax. Breathe."

Taking a few deep breaths, I felt my stomach slowly relax and the tension turned into a dull ache. Saleem sat on the floor next to me.

"I'm not going anywhere. Tell me. Start from the beginning," Mr. Mukherjee said, sitting back down.

I glanced at Saleem and he nodded encouragingly.

Looking into Mr. Mukherjee's face, I noticed his eyes were soft and gentle, like Bapuji's.

"Everybody lies . . ." I began.

*

When I'd finished, Mr. Mukherjee looked like he was in a daze. He produced his pocket watch and began to pace the classroom.

"Maybe he needs to go to the toilet too?" Saleem whispered in my ear, trying to make me laugh. But I wasn't in the mood for jokes.

I'd just told Mr. Mukherjee the truth and although it had been difficult, I felt a lot better. The weight that had been on my shoulders felt lighter. Mr. Mukherjee finally stopped pacing and sat back down. I could see his jaw clenching and his eyes looked tired.

"Bilal, I love your bapuji for all he's done for me—he fought to get me this job. When I heard he was going to die . . . Well, I was devastated, so God only knows how you must feel . . . Shame on me for not visiting him but having to see him like that, it's hard to bear." Mr. Mukherjee straightened in his chair and put on his glasses. "I'm not sure how I feel about what you're doing but I will say this. Because I love your bapuji, because I can understand why you, his son, would do this for him, because I can only guess how difficult this must be for you . . . I will help you. I'm not sure how yet but I will."

Saleem stirred next to me and let out a deep sigh of relief. *Mr. Mukherjee is going to help us!*

"Your secret is safe with me," he said gently.

Feeling overcome, I muttered thanks and made to leave but Saleem pulled me up short.

"Actually, Mr. Mukherjee, we need your help now. You see, we have to create a newspaper—by Friday . . ."

"You'd better tell me about it then," he said.

So Saleem told Mr. Mukherjee the whole story.

"Only you, Bilal! Why am I not surprised? But I said I would help and I will. How do you propose to create the newspaper?"

"It's all arranged. As long as we write it, Mr. Singh will print it for us," I replied.

"And why would he agree to that?" asked Mr. Mukherjee.

"We told him it was for a school project," chipped in Saleem.

Mr. Mukherjee widened his eyes and shook his head. "Clearly you two are ahead of the game here. I'll try my best to catch up."

185

Saleem stood up suddenly. "I have to leave," he said. He looked anxious.

"What is it?" I asked.

"Oh, nothing. I've just got to get home and help my bapuji with something. I'll pass by Chota and tell him you're with Mr. Mukherjee."

"Ah yes, the lookout. Trust that little rascal to worm his way out of school for this! He needs to be here more than anyone."

"Mr. Mukherjee, you said you'd help," I protested. "If Chota doesn't stay on the roof, we have no way of knowing who tries to visit Bapuji."

"OK, fine, I understand," he replied. "Tell Chota that we'll be at my house if he needs us. I need to get home before Mrs. Mukherjee comes looking for me."

Saleem agreed and quickly made his way out of the classroom. Mr. Mukherjee collected his papers and put them in his briefcase. He looked over at me.

"What is it? You still look worried. Is it Saleem?" he asked.

"Yes, he's hiding something but I don't know what."

"And is it your responsibility to understand and

solve everyone's problems?"

"No, it's not that. I just know something's wrong. Why won't he tell me? He tells me everything."

"Well, give him some time and maybe he'll come to you with whatever it is that's bothering him. He probably doesn't want to burden you with it at the moment," said Mr. Mukherjee, locking the school building and leading me down the street.

"Yes, maybe," I replied, unconvinced.

Perhaps Mr. Mukherjee was right. I had other things to worry about. Saleem would come to me if it was serious and so, for once, I wouldn't press him to tell me but would wait until he was ready to tell me himself.

Chapter 29

Mr. Mukherjee was very clever. He had graduated at the top of his class at every school he'd ever attended and his only dream was to be a teacher. Mr. Mukherjee knew that our motley bunch was always going to struggle with higher concepts and different types of thinking. It was a miracle that he'd managed to convince the market town committee that we needed a school at all but, luckily for Mr. Mukherjee, Bapuji was one of his strongest supporters. Subsequently the market-town traders had grudgingly accepted that it could be useful if their boys were good at math and learned about the history of their country, though that didn't stop many of them keeping the boys home to help at their stalls. Mr. Mukherjee was constantly visiting the stallholders to request that the boys stay at school and to say that their learning would be beneficial to the family, their business, and the community.

Mr. Mukherjee had a house on the other side of the street from the school. It was a lot bigger than ours and had four separate rooms, including a study, a dressmaking room, and a cooking room. The house felt warm and welcoming. The windows were wide open and golden sunlight lit up the room. The floor looked newly swept and soft rugs covered the floor. The cushions on the charpoi were freshly plumped and inviting. I sat down on a low chair and thought about our house as I looked around me. Our two musty rooms smelled of leather, books, dust, and something else. *I know what else.* The rooms smelled of death. But here the smell was different. People *lived* here.

I'll rest my head for a second just until Mr. Mukherjee comes back. What is that lovely smell? I remember that smell. It was Ma's favorite . . . What was it? Ah yes, I remember now—jasmine . . .

Feeling a hand stroking my head, I opened one blurry eye to see a woman in a white sari smiling at me . . . *Ma?*

"Bilal, it's time to wake up. Come and eat with us," said Mrs. Mukherjee.

Rubbing my eyes, I sat up. Mr. Mukherjee sat on the floor waiting and beckoned for me to sit next to him. Mrs. Mukherjee ruffled my hair and sat down on the floor too.

"Go and wash the sleep out of your eyes, Bilal," she said.

I walked outside and turned on the tap, splashing some cold water on my face. Then we ate in peaceful silence with Mrs. Mukherjee heaping things to eat on my plate. When we finished, we all sat back content with our bellies full.

Looking around and at Mr. and Mrs. Mukherjee, I felt a deep sadness settle on me. *This is everything I want but will never have.* Feeling tears sting my cheeks, I muttered that I had to use the toilet. Sitting in the toilet, I began to think of excuses I could use to leave. After a few minutes, Mrs. Mukherjee came to check on me.

"Bilal, are you OK? Come out, I've made some tea."

"Coming," I replied.

Walking back into the room, they were both

waiting for me. Mrs. Mukherjee handed me a cup of tea and sat me down. Mr. Mukherjee looked at me over the top of his glasses.

"Bapuji will be worrying about me—I'll have to go soon," I mumbled.

Mr. Mukherjee looked at Mrs. Mukherjee and raised his eyebrows. "You see, I told you," he said.

Looking from one to the other, I frowned. "What?" I asked.

"I told Mrs. Mukherjee that you are always moving," said Masterji. "You never sit or stand still. And when you do, even for a moment, you admonish yourself and get going, like you're trying to now."

Mrs. Mukherjee sat down next to me and took my hand.

"Bilal, Mr. Mukherjee has told me everything. He's told me what you've sworn to do," she said.

"You think I'm a fool, don't you?" I asked.

"No, I think you're a very brave boy. But no boy should have to take on this burden alone."

"But there's no one else," I replied quietly.

"What about your older brother? Surely he must take on some of the responsibility—some of the weight must be his."

"He has his own things to worry about. Anyway, I can't talk to him about this—he wouldn't understand," I replied.

"Until today, you thought *I* wouldn't understand," said Mr. Mukherjee. "You have to try him, Bilal."

"Next time Rafeeq comes home, I'll speak to him," I said. *If he ever comes home again, that is.*

Satisfied, Mrs. Mukherjee went into the cooking room and reappeared a few minutes later with some food for me to take home. I noticed that her eyes were red as if she'd been crying. I took the packet of food from her and muttered my thanks. She gathered me into her arms and held me tightly.

"I'll be OK, Auntie-ji. I'm a lot happier now that I've told you and each day it gets easier."

Easier to lie, easier to deceive, easier to only think about what I need to do.

Mr. Mukherjee stood at the door waiting for me.

"Bilal, tomorrow you won't be in school," he said.

"No?"

"No, you will be at home, working on this newspaper. I've written down a few guidelines for you to follow but I think *you* should write it. I'll help you, of course, but they should be your words."

"But, Masterji, I don't know the first thing about writing a news story. Where do I start? What will I say?"

"Start with the truth and then work your way from there," he replied.

He handed me several recent newspapers and a few pieces of paper with some notes.

"Here, take these, they'll give you an idea of how to begin. Then tomorrow night we'll work on it together."

I smiled slightly as I walked out of the house.

"I've just thought of a headline, Masterji," I said.

"What is it?"

"One India!" I replied.

"That's a very apt headline, Bilal," he said gently as he waved good-bye.

I walked home feeling more optimistic than I had for a long time.

Chapter 30

The next day I woke early, determined to make a start on the newspaper. Bapuji was still fast asleep as I sat sipping hot chai and enjoying the silence. But loud shouting shattered the peace.

"You son of a dog, we'll get you, you'll see."

"Of course you will, you son of a cockroach, of course you will."

Sneaking to the door, I peeked out and saw my brother approaching the house with his back turned, walking backward. He was still shouting at a couple of boys farther up the street.

Don't bring trouble here, Rafeeq, I thought. *The last thing we need is trouble on our street.* I watched the other boys carefully. *Why aren't they moving?* Then I realized. They were waiting to see which house he would go into. For a minute I panicked—if he came in here they'd know it was his house and there would be more trouble in the future. I clenched my fists. *Don't come here, don't you dare come here . . .* The other boys took a few steps forward but slowly. I felt torn. He was my brother after all. *I should go out to help him. But this is his problem, and brother or no he shouldn't bring trouble home.* Still undecided, I took a closer look at the other boys. They were smaller than my bhai and in a fight he would probably be able to match them or even give them a good hiding. Maybe that was the reason they weren't moving forward.

Then they picked up a few stones. My brother was only a few steps from the house. *Don't come in here, you fool!* He stopped right outside our house but didn't look inside. Instead he started hurling vicious insults at the other boys. Enraged, they threw stones at him but they were too far away to do any harm. Bhai taunted them a bit more and picked up a stone at his feet. As he did so, he flicked something into the house with his foot. It was a little stone with a piece of paper wrapped around it.

I read the note. *Meet me behind the barrels on the edge of the maidan at ten tonight.*

Sliding back to the door, I watched as my brother threw a few more stones and then calmly took a right turn and disappeared. The boys swore and ran after him. *They'll never catch him*, I thought. *He knows these streets better than anyone.*

Shaking my head, I settled back down to work. This evening I would tell him that we were better off without him. I'd make sure he understood what I was trying to do and I'd make it clear that he was never to come home again.

Chapter 31

Making my way to the barrels that evening, I was still angry. Why was it that every time I thought of my older brother I felt such a deep anger? It was not an anger where I wanted to hit him. The anger was all inside like a dull ache and it had a voice of its own. The voice wanted to ask him, *When did it change? When did we stop being brothers and start being strangers?* Bapuji used to be my brother's hero, too, but in the last few years Rafeeq had been different. He argued with Bapuji all the time and wouldn't come home. At first I didn't understand it, not for a long time. Bapuji never really argued and he never lost his temper. One day I understood that was why they argued. They argued because they were the opposite of each other, like heat and cold. Rafeeq was quick to temper and

Bapuji was always calm. No matter what Bapuji said, Bhai would argue anyway. The calmer Bapuji remained, the angrier Rafeeq became. It was even worse when they started to talk about politics. That's when he left home.

Realizing that I'd been almost running, I slowed down and took a deep breath.

It's no use being angry with my brother now. He made his choice and I made mine. As long as he doesn't interfere with what I'm trying to do, that's all that matters.

Approaching the stacked barrels, I skirted round to see if I could spot him but there were too many shadows in which he could be lurking. Suddenly, a hand shot out and grabbed me by the collar, pulling me into a dark spot.

"Get off me, will you?" I shouted.

"Shh, you'll alert the whole town, you idiot."

Breaking free of my brother's grasp and shoving him away, I turned to face him.

"I'm the idiot? I'm not the one being chased by thugs through the streets. I'm not the one who's bringing trouble home, am I? If I'm the idiot, what does that make you?"

Scowling, he lit a cigarette and sat on a barrel.

"No, of course, I forgot. You're a saint, aren't you, Bilal? Saint Bilal the Righteous. So young, yet so wise," he sneered, making smoke shapes as he spoke.

I took a deep breath. *Think of what I came here to do. Stay calm.*

"Why did you want to meet me?" I asked.

Irritated that he hadn't been able to annoy me, he pointed his cigarette at me. It was so dark I could barely make his face out as I followed the smoking butt of his cigarette. The dying light drew strange shapes in the air as I listened to his familiar voice. The same voice that used to read to me when I was small.

"I wanted to ask about the old man and also find out what arrangements you're making."

"Arrangements for what?" I asked.

"We spoke about this last time, Bilal. This whole place is going to the dogs. It's going to blow up very soon. You don't want to be here for that and neither does the old man."

"And I told you last time: I'm not going anywhere and neither is he."

"But, Bilal, they don't want us here. Why stay?"

"Because this is our home. This is where Bapuji

grew up. This is where we're from. I don't even know what this new Pakistan looks like. What would we do there?"

"That's not the point, the point is—"

"That *is* the point. For Bapuji and me anyway. You go if you want but we're staying here."

"You just don't understand. It's a bit difficult for me to come to the house right now but I'll find a way to come and speak with the old man. He might not want to move but he'll definitely make you go."

"Don't you dare come home," I said, almost in a whisper. "Not for this. You're not welcome anymore, Bhai."

"What the hell are you talking about, Bilal?"

Rafeeq sounded angry now as well as surprised. I could feel all my insides clenching into little balls of pain and the pressure almost made me cry out loud. *He needs to know. Tell him.* So I did.

After I'd told my brother everything, he sat perched on the barrel trying to understand. The cigarette in his hand smoldered until it reached his fingertips and burned him. Flinching then swearing, he flicked it away and stared after it. After a moment he lit another.

"You can't do that, Bilal," he said quietly.

"I am doing it. I'm not going to stop now," I replied with more confidence than I felt.

"But it's a lie, Bilal. You're lying to him. It's all a lie!" He almost shouted it.

Each time he said "lie," it felt like razors were cutting the insides of my stomach but it didn't matter. Not anymore.

"So it's a lie. But if we're talking about the truth— if *you're* the truth—then I prefer the lie."

"But how can you live with it, Bilal? Bapuji trusts you to look after him, to care for him, and to tell him the truth. How can you do this?"

"Easy—I love him. More than anything in the world. And if you had stayed, if you'd decided that being like him was enough, then *you'd* understand."

"I don't understand."

"I don't care. Just don't come home and don't bother us with your "truth." It's ugly and we want no part of it."

I could just make out his face in the moonlight. Tears glistened like little pearls rolling slowly down his cheeks.

"Bilal, it doesn't need to be like this . . ."

I looked away from his face before I lost my nerve. "Yes, it does."

I left Bhai sitting on the barrel, the cigarette burning close to his fingers. My last thought before I turned away was that if he wasn't careful it would burn him again—but if he hadn't learned from the first time there was nothing I could do.

Chapter 32
(20 days until Partition)

Saleem and I returned to Mr. Singh's printer's yard on the Friday feeling extremely pleased with ourselves. I had worked hard on the paper all week, spending the days writing and the evenings with Mr. Mukherjee. Mr. Singh opened the door and growled at us to come in. Taking our well-thumbed pieces of paper, he told us to come back in an hour after he had made them ready for printing.

While we waited, Saleem and I went by the rooftop and sat with Chota as he babbled on about a cockfight that was coming up. "But not just any fight. This will be the fight to end all cockfights . . ."

Promising Chota we'd be back later, we returned to Mr. Singh's house but we didn't feel as confident as we had earlier. I knocked on the door and held my breath.

The door swung open and a voice tore through the quiet.

"You two, get in here now."

Saleem shoved me forward and we walked into the house. Mr. Singh stood with his arms crossed. It was hard to tell if he was angry because Mr. Singh always looked angry.

"What in the guru's name is this?" he asked, pointing to our various bits of paper.

"Not the news you were expecting," said Saleem, the words escaping from his mouth before he'd had a chance to think.

"No, *not* the news I was expecting. Is this part of the assignment then? To write this, this . . ."

Go on, say it, Mr. Singh, you know what it is.

"These lies. What purpose does it serve to lie like this, eh?"

"We just want it to be different, that's all, Mr. Singh. Like a 'what if this happened,' you know," Saleem stammered, looking at me for support.

"There is a good reason. Will you print it?" I asked, my question cutting through Saleem's stammering.

"Print this . . . this drivel? No, I won't print it. It's fabrications, fictions, and lies. It'll be a waste of ink," replied Mr. Singh, sitting down on his battered stool and shaking his head.

"Fine," I said and walked out of his house as Saleem apologized to a stunned Mr. Singh.

Marching down the road, I stopped when I heard Saleem calling after me.

"What's the matter with you? If you'd explained it to him carefully, he might have gone for it," said Saleem exasperatedly.

"I worked hard on that paper, Sal, but he's right. It is all lies. Perhaps lies that are spoken aloud merely float away like leaves in the wind but writing them down creates a record of our lie. Our beautiful lie."

We heard shouting from behind us in the street and saw Mr. Singh striding toward us.

"Where are you running off to then?" he asked, breathing heavily.

"You said you won't publish it. What else is there to say?" I replied.

Saleem groaned.

Mr. Singh put his hands on his hips. "There is something more to this. Something you're not telling me." Narrowing his eyes, he looked closely at me. "Are you Gulam-bhai's son?"

For a moment I considered lying but Saleem elbowed me in the ribs and I muttered, "Yes."

Mr. Singh swore under his breath. "We need to talk," he said and ushered us back to his house, where he poured three cups of tea and signaled for us to sit down.

"I've known your bapuji ever since I was a small boy. He's older than me by a few years. We went to school together." He pointed to his printing machine and smiled. "Did you know that your bapuji helped me raise the money for this machine? No, I bet you didn't. He was always obsessed with books and printing of any kind, and he felt very strongly that this market town should be able to print its own news and leaflets. As I was the only one who could write and edit copy, naturally it fell to me to take this on but without a printer it was pointless. Your bapuji convinced the town committee to raise the money and lend it to me for a small machine, and so my business was born. Without his help, I'd still . . . I'm not sure what I'd be doing."

I could feel Saleem's eyes on me. I mouthed, "*What?*" at him and he mouthed back, "*Tell him.*"

If Saleem has his way, the whole town will know.

"Mr. Singh," I began, "if you know my bapuji as

well as you say you do, you might understand why I've written this paper ..."

After I'd finished explaining, Mr. Singh flicked through our pages and laughed, a deep guffaw echoing around the room. His face was softer now, the look in his eyes more gentle.

"Are you sure about this? I love your bapuji like a brother but is this the right thing to do?" he asked quietly.

"What's the alternative, Mr. Singh?"

He raised his eyes to the ceiling, saying a quick prayer under his breath: "Guru guide us ..."

Yanking the heavy ink-stained cloth from the machine, Mr. Singh turned to us with his hands on his hips.

"Leave it to me, it'll be printed by tomorrow. Go on now, I have to concentrate and put this clumsy copy into some kind of order. Get away with you."

Chapter 33

Standing in front of the three holies, I looked at my feet. The holy men had tried to visit Bapuji on four separate occasions and each time I'd managed to persuade them that he was asleep or unwell. However, this time they refused to go away. I knew that if I told the three holies, the whole market town, slowly but surely, would know the truth—or rather the lie—of what I was doing. Even so, if I told them it would make all our lives easier. Straightening up, I explained what I had resolved to do.

"You lied to us!" cried the reverend.

"This is morally unacceptable," said the imam.

"Your bapuji must know the truth," added the pandit.

"What would God think about all of this?" exclaimed the reverend.

"I don't know what God would say because I haven't asked him. But I think if I did ask him, he would understand," I said quietly.

Saleem stood to my right, glaring at the three holy men, and Manjeet stood defiantly in front of our doorway, picking his teeth with a little twig.

"Understand?" said the reverend. "But, my boy, this is an untruth, a lie. Your bapuji, he's dy—"

"Look, Pandit-ji, Imam-ji and Reverend-ji—" began Saleem, raising his voice.

"No, Saleem, it's OK—" I started.

"No, it isn't OK," he replied, standing in front of me. "It's not OK to come and do this outside Bilal's house. It's not OK to accuse people of being something they're not, and it's not OK to . . . to . . ."

"Sal . . ." I tried again.

"So please go away and leave us to do what we have to do," Saleem continued.

"Baghvan, guide these boys to the truth," said the pandit.

"Allah forgive them . . ." started the imam.

I watched appreciatively as Saleem shouted at the

209

three holies while they wrung their hands and tutted at me. Manjeet continued picking his teeth, amusedly looking on as Saleem growled and snapped at them. Eventually I put a hand on Saleem's shoulder. Turning around, he stopped shouting and stepped back. Looking at each of the three men in turn, I held up my hands. They stopped talking. I could taste the disapproval on the tips of their tongues.

"You want me to tell the truth?" I asked.

As one, they all muttered yes and nodded their assent.

"Are you sure that's the best thing to do?" I asked.

Again, they all agreed with a jangle of beads, chains, and heavy cloth.

"OK then. Pandit-ji, when you first came here to do your job, you told everybody that you had been taught by a famous guru in Delhi but everyone knows that you came from Chennai and have never been to Delhi."

"No, that's not quite . . ." the pandit spluttered.

"Imam-ji, you tell everyone that your son works in an important government job but we all know that he's a dacoit and lives in a village near Batalia."

"Well, no. I mean, yes. He does live near Batalia but he's not . . ."

"And you, Reverend-ji, when was the last time somebody came to confession?"

"Ah, well, it's been a while. It's been a bit slow. We're a small community . . ."

"Reverend-ji, perhaps it's something to do with the fact that when you get really drunk, you like to tell whoever will listen the confessions of your sheep."

"Flock. You mean flock," replied the reverend.

"You know what I mean," I replied. "You all do."

Saleem and Manjeet were both standing with their mouths open, looking at me. Pushing past them I opened the door and gestured to the three men.

"So, please come in. I'm sure Bapuji would love to hear your truth," I said.

The three holies stood rooted to the spot in the quiet street.

"We don't want to disturb him if he's sleeping . . ." began the reverend.

"Yes, he needs his rest. It would do him no good to jabber on with us three old men," followed the imam.

"Quite, quite. You give him our best, Bilal. God give him succor," said the reverend.

The pandit closed his eyes in prayer. The imam lifted his hands to the sky and swayed as he mouthed a prayer. The reverend flicked his rosary beads and looked into the distance.

"Thank you for coming," I said.

"Think nothing of it, my boy. Tell him he's in our prayers," replied the reverend.

Watching them go, I slid down against the wall and sat down.

"Bilal, that was . . ." began Saleem.

"I knew that sooner or later people would find out about what I was doing, but I don't feel good about what I just did," I replied.

"But, Bilal, you . . ." spluttered Saleem, struggling to find the words.

"You told them what they needed to hear, Bilal," said Manjeet quietly. "If they didn't want to hear it they shouldn't do what they do. And they definitely shouldn't tell other people what to do."

"Thanks, Manjeet, that makes me feel a little better," I replied.

Manjeet nodded and slid down next to me. Saleem still stood, trying to find the right words but, rolling his eyes, he gave up and slid down too.

"Did you see the looks on their faces?" said Saleem, snickering.

"It was very funny," replied Manjeet.

"It's hard to describe, it's almost as if they . . . I don't know," said Saleem.

"Almost as if they were surprised at hearing the truth said aloud," finished Manjeet.

"I can understand that," I said, shrugging my shoulders.

"What do you mean?" asked Saleem.

"If you tell a lie long enough, it becomes real. Then the lie no longer exists and all you're left with is your version of the truth."

"It must have been some surprise to hear it said out in the open like that then," replied Manjeet.

"It must've been like a kick in the teeth," I agreed.

"Do you think you'll ever feel like that?" asked Saleem.

"No, I will never feel like that. Never," I said.

"Still, we managed to get the newspaper sorted. Has he read it yet?" asked Saleem.

Mr. Singh had made an exact replica of a newspaper for us, printed on a particular paper so that it would even feel like a real newspaper. Even he had been pleased with how well it had turned out—he had brought the paper to the house himself, proud he had done his bit.

"I'm going to wait until this evening then give it to him so he can read it in the candlelight just before he falls asleep," I said.

"Think he'll notice?" asked Manjeet.

"I don't think so. He sleeps a lot nowadays and when he is awake he's not quite sure where he is. Sometimes he seems to think I'm Ma . . ."

"Do you want me to stay with you?" asked Saleem.

"No, no, go on home. I'll meet you on the rooftop tomorrow as usual," I replied.

As Manjeet and Saleem slipped away, I watched the light change. Moving into the house and closing the door behind me, I gathered up the newspaper. Bapuji was lying in bed with his eyes open, staring at the ceiling.

"Bapuji, you're awake! How are you feeling?"

Bapuji looked at me in surprise. *He's not quite sure where he is.*

"Look, Bapuji, I've brought you a newspaper," I said.

Coming back to himself, Bapuji perked up and smiled gratefully. Taking the paper from me, he held it close to his eyes, squinting in the candlelight. I sat on the bed, trying not to fidget as he read it. When he finally put the paper down, he looked at me and beamed.

"I told you it would be OK, Bilal," he said happily.

"You were right, Bapuji. Everything will be OK now," I replied. I took the paper from him, prepared his medicine, and settled him down for the night.

Chapter 34

A week later, we sat on the rooftop as the market gradually woke as if from a deep slumber. Fewer and fewer stalls dared to open these days. Those that did were owned by resolute traders determined to retain their normal routine.

Normal, I thought. *What is normal anyway? I'm pretty sure it's not hating people so much you want to kill or maim them. That's not normal.*

Looking around, I could feel the tension in our group. Saleem, whose optimism was usually infectious, sat sullenly on the edge of the rooftop looking out into the distance, his legs hanging over the side but not dangling carefree like they used to. I knew he still wasn't telling me something. He had a secret too and it had punctured his hopefulness. Manjeet sat slightly away from us whittling a piece of wood. He had worn it down to a nub but still he continued to slice it absentmindedly. His mind wasn't completely here either. Over the last week, Manjeet had become more and more withdrawn. I felt him watching me and when I turned to look at him and smile, he looked away. As the sun came up, we were all exposed to its light and what we saw of each other made us look away.

Chota came bounding up the stairs and shook us out of our thoughts. He looked from face to face and saw the unease but that had never stopped Chota in the past and it wasn't about to now.

"The cockfight is this afternoon! It's between two of the biggest, nastiest birds I've ever seen. There'll be lots of people there. We have to go!"

Manjeet stopped whittling his little piece of wood and, looking down at it as if for the first time, threw it away.

"Cockfights are for grown men. If they catch us they'll tell us to go away," said Manjeet.

"No, it'll be OK. My uncle will look after us. Anyway there'll be so many people coming, they won't even notice us," replied Chota excitedly, hopping from foot to foot.

"What's the fight in aid of? And why are so many people going to it?" Saleem asked.

"I don't know but I went past old man Pondicherry and overheard him saying something about it to Anand. I didn't understand what, though," said Chota, shrugging his shoulders.

Going right to the edge of the building, I looked over to where old Pondicherry usually sat and although I couldn't make him out, I saw his stick leaning against a barrel.

Chota was beside himself with excitement by now and trying to spread some of his enthusiasm to us.

"So? Are we going or not?" he asked.

Saleem looked at me and shook his head. "There'll be trouble . . ." he said.

"So, what's new?" replied Manjeet, standing up and stretching his long legs.

Manjeet and Saleem had livened up a bit now that Chota was here. I nodded my head.

Chota's face lit up. "I hope it's a bloody fight," he squealed.

I said that I was off to see old man Pondicherry and that I'd be back shortly to meet up with them before the fight.

I found Pondicherry-ji sitting and staring out with sightless eyes on to the maidan. I felt reluctant to disturb him.

"Ah, Bilal. Stop dawdling, boy, and come closer," he said, beckoning me with his wrinkled hand.

I went and sat on the barrel next to him and looked out at whatever it was he was looking at, or rather not looking at. I was never quite sure what Mr. Pondicherry did or didn't see.

"Have you heard about this cockfight this afternoon?"

"It's hard not to have heard about it, Bilal. It's all anybody's talking about," he replied.

"Why? It's only another bird fight, isn't it?"

"We're just like animals really," said Mr. Pondicherry, shaking his head. "We can smell blood now and that raw smell appeals to the worst part of us. Our dark side. It makes us do things we'd normally only ever think about."

"But what's that got to do with the cockfight?"

"The mob, child. The mob will be there and they'll be looking for a sign," he sighed, his chin dipping to his chest.

"Will you be going?" I asked.

"Even though I can't see, I'll be there," he replied.

"But why?" I asked incredulously.

"Because I'm just an animal too. And if we're nearing the end, I need a sign," he whispered. "Now off with you, go on." He shooed me away.

"I don't need a sign—I know the end is close," I replied and left the old man to look out on to the empty maidan.

Chapter 35

Back on the rooftop, Saleem came and stood next to me, putting his arm around my shoulder. I put my arm around him and couldn't help chuckling.

"What are you chuckling at, shorty?" he asked.

"You, you fool! You've been a bit moody lately . . ."

"Me? Look who's talking!" said Saleem. "You're the one who's always gazing off into the distance with a strange look in your eye. We're all half expecting you to start spouting some Tagore or Kabir at any moment."

Shoving Saleem away from me, I cuffed him lightly on the head.

"Oh, look!" I pointed at the stream of people below, all moving in one direction. "There'll be a lot of people at this fight, Sal."

"But we're little—we'll get to the front quickly," he replied, grinning.

"That's not what I meant," I said and looked over at the cemetery. "There's something Mr. Pondicherry said, about the mob . . ."

"Well, we'll never find out what he means by sitting here on the rooftop. And you've got Mr. Mukherjee sitting with your bapuji all day so we've got nothing to worry about. Let's get going!" Jumping up, Saleem ran down the stairs.

We watched as wave after wave of people made their way to the cemetery off the main square. Cockfights were always held in the cemetery. It was just the way it was. I'd asked Bapuji about it once and he'd said that the elders decided that it would do no good to have fights in the marketplace but it was acceptable if they were in the cemetery. Then looking at me and smiling, he'd added, "It also means council members can get down there and place a bet like everyone else without their wives finding out."

We joined the wave of people and were instantly swept up into the tide. As ever, Manjeet led the way, his orange turban bobbing along in front of us. Saleem hung close on my right and I held on tightly to Chota on my left to stop him getting distracted and disappearing into the crowd. It was slow going as the maidan began to fill with people from all sides. Gradually, we came to a standstill and I could feel the body of the crowd or—what had old man Pondicherry called it?—the mob. Embedded in the center, we were held fast. We were all swaying, this mass of humanity tuned to one another. I closed my eyes. From one side pulsed anger, violence, and the need for blood. Swaying in another direction, I felt tranquility, peace, and the need for meditation. Right in front of me, I felt impatience, anxiety, and the need to discover the outcome no matter what it was.

Opening my eyes, I struggled to readjust to the light and sound. Manjeet's orange turban blurred in front of me and bled into the crowd. Blinking, I tried to clear my head of this strange vision but it just made it worse. Everywhere I looked, colors were bleeding into each other. Red scarves bled into white dhotis, silver bangles melted into dark brown skin, azure sky dissolved into white clouds and dripped into the crowd. It was the most beautiful thing I'd ever seen. We were all part of one swaying movement pushing forward together. There was no beginning or end. Like the banyan tree, the mother had been swallowed and only her children were left. Was this the mob old man Pondicherry had described? I had thought that it would be ugly and destructive but I could see euphoria in everybody's eyes.

My feet barely touched the ground as we began to move steadily forward. Flowing through the gates we split into a trickle to navigate the small paths between the hodgepodge of graves. We slowly moved through the bowl-shaped cemetery toward the little dirt circle that had been cleared at the bottom of the hill. The mass of people surrounding the circle was growing before our eyes.

Manjeet turned to me and shook his head. "There's no way we can go any farther than here," he said.

"I can find a way," replied Chota, bristling impatiently. I let go of his arm and he shoved his way to Manjeet. Showing his teeth, he cackled, "Follow me." And with that he pushed forward.

We shadowed him. I was directly behind Chota and struggling to keep up. He found gaps where there were none. When he came up against a wall of humanity, he found a way under it or around it and in one case he even climbed over a man. We all did our best to follow but I couldn't see Manjeet's orange turban anywhere. *Where is he?* Panicking, I tried to stop but Chota clung tightly on to my hand, squeezing it hard as we slowly made our way through. Chota wasn't satisfied until he had dragged us right to the front.

Finally, my eyes started to focus. There were a number of people in the middle of the circle who I recognized from around the town. One of them was Chota's uncle, who clearly had a senior role in proceedings because he wore a black armband and was speaking to two men who both listened intently to him. *Where are the roosters?* I couldn't see the cages anywhere. The circular space in the middle was becoming smaller as everybody pressed forward and Chota's uncle signaled to some large men to hold the surge back. Everywhere you looked, you could see people on tiptoes trying to glimpse what was happening. Some had brought wooden crates and were teetering on them, looking down on to the dusty circle. Some resourceful bands of people had even built a mound of earth on which to stand. I remembered a similar scene in a book I'd read once about ancient Rome in the time of the Caesars. A time when people would enter an arena to watch two gladiators fight to the death. Well, this was our arena and it was fitting that death was all around. For a second, I wondered if all the spirits of the dead would be watching too. Looking up and around, I could sense something in the air. Chota's uncle had stopped speaking to the two owners of the birds and they both turned and disappeared into the milling crowd—there one instant and swallowed the next. The pressure of the mob was such that it was hard to stay on our feet. I locked elbows with Saleem and Chota and we braced ourselves as each wave of movement hit us harder than the last. At times, I was lifted off my feet as a wave seared through us. The mob was becoming impatient.

The two bird owners returned holding cages covered in dark cloth. An old man, who had been sitting on an upturned crate at the edge of proceedings, slowly went to stand in the center of the circle and raised his hand. The gesture knifed its way through the crowd and spread itself right to the edges of the cemetery. It was a call for quiet. He signaled for both men to come forward with their birds. The silence lengthened as the men retrieved the roosters and approached the old man. Their heads covered with dark cloth, the birds weren't yet aware of their surroundings. The men stood opposite each other waiting for a gesture from the old man. Flicking his wrist, he motioned for the pieces of cloth to be flung back and the birds were held aloft. The crowd erupted, the sound and the fury raising us right off our feet. The birds were held a few inches apart, beak to beak, being whipped into a frenzy. Finally, at a signal from the old man, they were released.

The birds flew at each other, tearing and snapping. After a furious first exchange, they became wary and began circling. I watched as the dust that had been kicked up at the start began to settle. *They're both so different*, I thought. The larger bird, the Ghan, was a rusty-brown color with a golden bill. Strutting around, its yellow spurs looked dull in the bright light but sharp and vicious. The smaller Aseel was a Rampur, solid black, its crimson bill swinging left to right like a pendulum. His spurs were small but jagged and pointed. The birds stopped circling and closed on each other again. The Ghan went straight for the

227

Rampur's neck but the smaller bird was nimble and dodged the strike. Already, you could sense a pattern to the contest. The bigger bird pursued the smaller bird around the dusty ring, its strong, curved neck and short beak tensed and ready to strike. The Rampur, realizing it was not as strong, employed a counter strategy, nipping at the larger bird and then darting away, banking on the Ghan wasting energy in chasing him. It was a dangerous strategy because it only needed one sledgehammer strike to connect and the smaller Rampur would be in trouble. It was a contest the mob could relate to.

The noise from the crowd reverberated through our deadly amphitheater and sent vibrations right through my spine. The roar of the mob was the ultimate release. The whole town had been holding its breath for weeks now and here it was all around me: raw rage, and relief at finally having let go. One way or another the mob wanted blood. Time slowed to a standstill. Everywhere I looked, faces and bodies were contorted into twisted, ugly shapes raw with emotion. Mouths were open, dark maws emanating a piercing sound. These were people I had known my entire life but in this arena we were all strangers, as if we had been told to leave our humanity at the cemetery gates.

Wrenching my eyes from the contest, I looked across and saw old man Pondicherry leaning on his stick directly opposite me, staring into the ring. I understood that it was no benefit being blind in this place at this moment. Old man Pondicherry was a storyteller and this scene in his imagination would be a lot worse than ours.

Saleem grabbed me tight and pulled me in close.

"They're not stopping, they dare not risk it—not with this mob," he shouted over the noise.

"What do you mean?" I asked.

"Usually they stop the contest, give the birds a break, but today it's a fight until the end. To the death, Bilal," Saleem shouted, his eyes reflecting the bloodlust of the crowd.

Of course it's to the end. Nothing less will do today.

Only minutes had passed but already it felt like an eternity. The Rampur was still set on evading the attentions of the Ghan, who was now tiring a little. The strikes were still vicious but were less frequent. Frustrated, the Ghan rushed at the Rampur only to land awkwardly. Finally seeing his opportunity, the

Rampur threw himself at the exposed back of the Ghan and cut him deeply. The squeal of pain that emanated from the Ghan's throat tore through the crowd and, for a minute, there was a hush as the larger bird turned and for the first time in the bout retreated a few steps. Tired and hurt, the Ghan shuffled sideways, watching the Rampur warily. I could feel my heart drumming in my chest. Suddenly, like a firework, the mob erupted once more. This was like every battle the mob had ever fought. Against poverty, against hardship, against fate. A fight against every time they had been told, "This is just the way it is, so accept it and make the best of what you have."

Strutting and more confident, the Rampur was now the stalker and pursued the Ghan around the circle. Stumbling and in pain, the Ghan clumsily moved away from striking distance but the Rampur was not to be denied and landed blow after blow on the Ghan's exposed neck and back. We were hauled off our feet again as the mob sensed the end and pushed forward. A tidal wave of human anguish and anger. The Rampur bobbed his head, sensing the killing strike. The birds leapt at each other, trying to land the final telling blow. In his haste the Ghan slipped in one final desperate attack and landed a vicious blow. Flinching but turning quickly, the Rampur finally saw the exposed neck of the Ghan and brought his beak down with all his force. Both birds spun away and retreated. The Ghan's black coat was streaked with crimson. The Rampur stood upright, eyeing the Ghan who, swaying, fell to the dust. A huge cheer shot into the sky as word spread like wildfire through the crowd. The Rampur tottered on his thin legs and, lifting his head slowly, took in the arena. Taking a step backward, he fell sideways. Letting go of Saleem and Chota, I took a step forward and fell to my knees. *No!* I could see that the Rampur's eyes were open to the sky. Glistening, they were the color of pearls.

Chapter 36

As word of the Rampur's fall spread through the crowd, I turned to see the human wave behind us crash and break into a thousand little pieces. Chota slammed into me, closely followed by Saleem, as the circle of humanity broke. Grabbing them both, we scrabbled away from the onslaught. I saw the owner of the Rampur cradling the Aseel in his hands. Fights and arguments were breaking out everywhere. Old man Pondicherry still stood in the same spot. Dragging Chota and Saleem with me, I ran to him.

"Pondicherry-ji, we have to get out of here! Now!" I told him.

Turning to me and smiling tenderly, he said, "No. I have to witness this, Bilal. For my sins, I am a witness. Leave now, and don't look back. Never look back."

Waving, he trotted away.

Screaming at him, I told him to stop but he didn't turn around.

Saleem grabbed my arm and pulled me away, leading us up the hill toward the cemetery gates.

My vision swam again and colors started to bleed into one another—but it was no longer beautiful. It was ugly. Men set upon each other with rocks and stones. Others ripped branches from trees and used them to batter at figures cowering in the dirt. As we climbed over graves, we saw others who had brought knives and machetes and were cutting swaths through fleeing men. Crimson streaks bled into white cotton and for an instant the mix of colors was beautiful again.

The hill became steeper and we had to use our arms to clamber up. We could smell smoke. As we climbed, a hand grabbed my leg.

"Help me, help me! I don't want to die," screamed a voice. But I couldn't see his face, just a hand that scrabbled through the dirt and held on to me.

Chota kicked at it, shouting. Kicking out as well, I dislodged the hand and stared as it disappeared. Chota nudged me and we continued to climb only to be confronted with a wall of fire. Holding fast to the muddy slope, we turned to see a vision of hell. There was fire and black smoke clouds everywhere. People crawled on their bellies toward loved ones who lay unmoving in the midst of graves. Others pursued victims through the smoke and upon catching them, pounded them until they stopped screaming. My vision still swimming in among the blood and smoke, I saw color hemorrhaging. All around were strewn flowers. Red roses bled into yellow flowers. White petals sunk into brown mud. Pink petals were kicked up into the air and rested on motionless bodies. I looked up to see Chota and Saleem standing over me.

"It's not a dream, is it?" I whispered. "Did I faint?"

Saleem hauled me up and nodded. "I think so. We turned and you were lying on the ground."

Chota scrambled up the hill and whistled down at us. "Come on, we're close to the top. It all looks quiet," he said, waving us up.

Saleem pushed me forward and we climbed up to where Chota sat, his head peeping over the edge of the low incline. Peering through the gloom there was little indication anybody was still alive.

"What do you think—" began Chota, only to be

stopped by Saleem.

"Shh! What was that?"

Listening carefully, we all heard the sounds of shuffling and scratching directly in front of us. A figure suddenly emerged, disappearing just as quickly. *There!* To our right, another scrabbling sound and another apparition appeared, his hand on his head, vanishing into a billowing smoke cloud. All around us now we could hear sounds of movement and other sounds, wrenched out of human throats. Sounds of sobbing, pain, and a low keening that cut through the smoke.

Chota grimaced and covered his ears. "Is that a dying cat or something?" he said, making a face.

Putting his arm around him, Saleem said nothing and looked at me.

What now?

We had little choice but to go through the gloom. Still watching me, Saleem gritted his teeth determinedly and blew out his cheeks. Removing his scarf, Saleem tore a long strip and pulled us close.

"Tie this around your waists, that way we can't be cut off from each other. It's not far now. Don't stop, no matter what, just keep walking." Taking another determined step, Saleem pulled us forward into the gloom.

Instantly we were blind. Trying to carefully pick our way over and around graves, we stumbled slowly forward. Shapes flitted in and out of the gloom around us. We walked for what seemed a long time but it is difficult to gauge the passing of time when you are holding your breath.

Saleem suddenly stopped. Signaling for us to do the same, he went down on one knee.

"I think we're lost," he said, bowing his head. "We should be close to the path leading into the main part of the cemetery but I have no idea where we are."

"It's not your fault. Look, the smoke will clear soon and we'll be able to see where we have to go. Maybe if we sit here for a minute . . ."

I knew as soon as I spoke that that was a bad idea. Sooner or later one of those apparitions would stumble over us and then who knows what they would do. Saleem understood and straightened up again.

"I think it's best if we keep moving," he said.

Taking tentative steps, we moved on. The keening sound was now closer to us and continued to ring in our ears. Chota was bent low, eyes flitting left and right trying to pin down each sound. I'd never seen him so panicked. Saleem had slowed to a crawling pace. A man came running right toward us, bursting through the cloying smoke, screaming. Horrified, we watched him hold his face—or what was now left of it—his flesh burned and blistered. Saleem hurriedly pulled us out of his path. We stared as he flew past, clothes still smoldering. As he disappeared, his scream mingled with the keening to create such a heart-rending cacophony that we all kneeled down and covered our ears. When we could no longer hear his screams, Saleem and I stood up and felt a tug from the cloth binding us together because Chota still cowered on the ground, a haunted look in his eyes.

"Chota, Chota? It's OK, he's gone. We can go on," I said, kneeling back down next to him.

"Go where? This isn't our world. Where are we going to go?" he asked.

"OK, OK, we'll wait here for a while, Chota, OK," I said soothingly.

Chota pulled his knees in and sat rocking back and forth, wild eyes scanning the murk around us. Saleem still stood peering into the gloom trying to make out the cemetery gates. Feeling a sharp pull on the knot at my waist, I pulled him back.

"What is it, Saleem? What do you see?"

"I ... I thought I saw somebody but he's gone again," he replied. "There he is again! Mr. Pondicherry! Mr. Pondicherry! Here! We're over here. *Mr. Pondicherry?*"

Out of the billowing smoke clouds came old man Pondicherry, his stick sweeping the hard earth in front of him.

"Saleem, boy, is that you?" he asked, stopping in front of us.

"Mr. Pondicherry, we're lost and don't know the way out," I said quickly.

"Bilal too, and who else do you have with you?" he asked, his sightless gaze settling on Chota.

"Chota's here too," replied Saleem.

"Well, you can't stop here. There's no telling who's haunting this gloom. Follow me."

Scrambling to our feet, we followed closely behind as he led the way, his stick tapping on broken branches, heavy rocks, and cracked headstones. The apparitions continued to move around us but the keening wail began to fade as we moved forward. Just as suddenly, the cemetery gates loomed above us and we walked through, relieved and bone-weary.

"Somebody tipped a large barrel of oil and lit it," Mr. Pondicherry muttered to himself. "With all that dry brush on the ground . . ."

"How did you find your way out?" I asked.

Mr. Pondicherry sighed. "I'm an old man, Bilal. Any friends I ever had are either buried or have been spread to the four winds."

"I don't understand—" I began.

"When you get old, boy, the only place where you can visit your friends is the cemetery. I've been there so many times, I could find my way out walking backward, gagged, and blindfolded."

Once in the market square, Mr. Pondicherry located his usual barrel in the shade and sat down. He looked out into the distance and shook his head.

"I can still smell smoke," he muttered under his breath. "Go now. Before long this whole square will be haunted by ghosts both dead and alive," he said firmly, waving his stick. "Go home!"

Chapter 37

Ignoring Mr. Pondicherry's advice, we ran to our rooftop, rushed up the stairs, and slumped down on the well-worn bags of rice. We all knew this would be the first place Manjeet would come. We sat in silence contemplating what we had seen and heard. A few minutes later, just as we were wondering if Manjeet would appear, his orange turban poked through the doorway. We all jumped up as we saw his blood-splattered white tunic. Saleem was the first to reach him and grabbed his arm.

"Manjeet, is this blood?"

"It's . . . it's not mine," he replied, throwing himself down on to a sack of rice.

"What happened?" I asked.

"After I lost you, I made my way as close as I

could to the front. I was almost opposite you and tried calling to you but I was drowned out by the noise. When the ring of people broke it hit us hard on the other side and I tried to get out of the way. I saw lots of people fall and be trampled. I tried to find you but it was mayhem and I had no idea if you'd still be in the same place. I saw barrels of oil being tipped over and lit on the hill. The wall of fire was directly in front of me and I thought if I tried to go round it I could find my way out of the cemetery that way. I knew I needed to go up the hill but that meant going through the fire. I couldn't see five yards in front of me for all the smoke. People were rushing at the fire and jumping through the flames. I took a few steps back and ran at the fire. I came out the other side not too hurt but right into a vision of . . . It was . . . awful."

Manjeet paused and squeezed his eyes shut, pressing his knuckles into his temples. "Men with sticks and knives were trying to kill each other . . . burn each other . . . I tried to get away but men kept rushing at me with sticks and knives . . . I *had* to defend myself . . . What else could I have done?" asked Manjeet, looking up at me, bloodshot eyes reliving the nightmare.

Sitting down next to him, I put my arm around his shoulder.

"Nothing. It wasn't your fault, Manjeet. You did nothing wrong."

"Bilal's right. You managed to escape and that's the main thing," said Saleem.

"But they would have killed me if I hadn't . . . They saw my turban and came at me calling me terrible things. I even recognized some of them . . . What else could I have done?" Manjeet asked again, imploring me to give him an answer he could bear to hear.

I could think of nothing to say. Manjeet had killed a man but he was still my friend. I wanted to help him, to say the right words that would make it better for him. Instead all I could do was sit with my arm around him while he quietly wept.

Smoke was still thick in the air as we sat on the rooftop in silence, each of us with our own terrible thoughts. It wasn't long until we heard the wails begin around the town.

Standing up, Manjeet looked at us with glazed eyes and, mumbling to himself, moved toward the stairs. Without looking back, he disappeared before we could stop him.

Saleem looked over the side of the building.

"He looks like he's going home," said Saleem to no one in particular. Turning to me, he sucked in a deep breath. "I'd better be getting home too. My ma will be worrying."

"Yes, we should all go home, I suppose," I replied absentmindedly.

Moving over to Chota, Saleem lifted him to his feet and went to shift him.

"I'll see you both later," I said.

"I'll try to get out tonight if I can," replied Saleem, still holding on to a dazed-looking Chota.

"Saleem . . ." I began.

"Yes, I know, we'll talk later. Get home now. If your bapuji's woken up he'll be wondering where you are."

"You're probably right."

"We'll meet later," said Saleem, propping up Chota and disappearing through the doorway.

I watched them stumble down the stairs.

Chapter 38

The next day, we all sat on the rooftop looking at the deathly quiet market. A vague memory nudged at me and I remembered seeing in encyclopedias photos of animal carcasses, bits of torn flesh still clinging on to the remains of jutting bones. Closing my eyes, I dredged up what the encyclopedia said next. After the predators had had their fill, next came the scavengers, the laughing hyenas. Well, the predators had been and the carcass of our town was revealed for all to see. Looking up at the sky, I saw clouds gathering. *What's next? The scavengers.* I'd never heard a hyena laugh but I'd seen pictures of a pack and knew it would be an ugly thing.

Looking around the rooftop, I could sense that we were no longer the same group we had once been.

Manjeet sat with his back to the market, avoiding looking over at the cemetery, perhaps in the hope that if he didn't see it he could learn to forget the Aseel fight and the fire. Turbaned head bowed, I noticed that the bright orange material had lost its glow.

Chota sat in his usual place, feet dangling over the edge. Even though everything had changed, Chota refused to.

Saleem sat the farthest away from me. I wanted to go and sit next to him. To ask him whether something was wrong. For him to tell me what was on his mind. But I was tired. Weary of bearing my own secret and unwilling to shoulder his. If I'd known what I know now, I'd have walked over, sat next to him and, putting my arm around him, spoken with him. Perhaps we would have laughed together one last time. But the moment passed. I didn't know then that I would never see Saleem again.

Chapter 39
(7 days until Partition)

There were two things about myself I had begun to hate. Not the usual things. I didn't want to be taller or good-looking or better at cricket. But there were two things I wished I had never been born with.

Firstly, my awareness of others. How many times had I been having a perfectly good time only for it to be ruined by my acute sense of the people around me? Often, I would sit and tune in to facial gestures, hand movements, and the subtle flicker of eyes and mouths. Some days, I didn't even feel I was really there as I sat among friends or family but rather that I was acting as a conduit for everyone else's feelings. My second hated thing was my "skill" for spotting what's not said. The words behind the words. This was my speciality. And that's when premonition takes over. *Premonition*. It was a word I'd learned recently. Premonition was the dull ache in my stomach, the pain behind my eyes, the overwhelming feeling that something bad was going to happen but only I could feel it. And on this day I realized something. That these two are related.

As I walked to Saleem's house, I imagined asking Doctorji to use his scalpel to cut out my two defining character traits. I felt Doctorji making the first cut and flipping the top of my head open, and I saw my brain revealed. It would all be clearly marked for safe removal. Just like that, Doctorji could remove those two hated cousins and flip my scalp back on. And I would be free. Free of always sensing everything around me, free to live each day without worrying that something bad was going to happen. Free to just be.

Shaking my head to clear this vision, I took a deep breath and continued toward Saleem's house. Houses in this area were built almost on top of one another but it was unnaturally quiet. A solitary old woman sat on her haunches to the side of her house, washing clothes. I stopped to watch her as she slapped the cloth against a raised stone. She was scrubbing it to death. Flinging it aside, she picked up another piece of material. A white sari. Raising it over her head, ready to slap it against that hard rock, she stopped as she brought it down and held it close to her chest. As she held the bunched-up material, I saw the white sari was streaked with red.

Approaching the clearing where Saleem's house stood, I felt the leaden weight of my thoughts. *Why did I come? I knew what I'd find but I still came. Why? Because I have to know. I always need to know. No matter how bad it becomes, I have to see it for myself.*

I walked through the door. There was nobody there. Saleem and his family were gone.

They'd left little behind. A few pots, an old broken charpoi, and a few bolts of dusty-blue material leaning against the far wall. This was Saleem's secret. He had known weeks ago that his family was preparing to leave but he had hidden it from me. Thinking back, I could remember all the times he'd tried to tell me but I'd been distracted.

I walked out to the yard toward the well and the end of the path. We had spent the summers here, doling out water to the surrounding houses and soaking each other to keep cool. It's where we had sat and done our schoolwork, lounging in the shade of the peepul tree. Looking up at the tree, I narrowed my eyes to see if our little den was still intact. Climbing up, I scrambled through the branches and there it was, made of bamboo we'd lashed together with bits of twine and string. Dropping down to my knees, I crawled into the box-shaped den and looked out on to the small yard. Curling into a tight ball, I pushed my face into the musty straw. A part of my mind wondered if anybody could hear me crying but it was a stupid thought. I knew there was nobody left to hear.

Chapter 40
(5 days until Partition)

A pigeon shot up into the sky. *Somebody is coming.* I shimmied up the two-story building opposite our house, clambered on to the roof and looked down on to the maze of houses. I saw Chota a few streets away on our rooftop lookout, waving his arms at me. Waving back, I tried to spot who was angling their way toward our house. Whoever it was had picked a good time to come—it was almost dark and the streets were barely lit. *There!* A flash of white, the figure moving fast, flitting in and out of the streets. *There again!* Whoever it was knew these streets well enough to navigate at speed. Chota was still waving his arms around frantically, making odd gestures, and pointing at me. *What is he doing?*

Making my way quickly back down the side of the

building, I went to stand outside our house. It didn't matter who it was, I'd deal with them. I looked down the dark street and waited, narrowing my eyes. A hand on my shoulder made me spin round in surprise.

"How's it going, little brother?"

"What—" I began to splutter.

"Shh! Before you start jabbering, let's get in. I made sure nobody followed me here and even if they tried, I'd have lost them by now. Come on," Bhai said, stepping inside the house before I could stop him.

Following him in, I grabbed him by the arm.

"What are you doing here? I thought we agreed you wouldn't come here and bring your troubles with you," I said, keeping my voice low.

"No, *you* decided that I wouldn't come here. I never agreed to any such thing. Now, stop getting angry and calm down. I just want a quick word with the old man," Bhai replied, taking a step forward.

Holding my hands out in front of me, I stood in front of him.

"No. Bapuji's sleeping and if you want to talk to him about moving away then you'd best leave. He doesn't need to hear that and neither do I."

My brother took a step back and lit a cigarette.

"It's getting serious out there, Bilal. How long do you think you can stay here before a mob finds you and flushes you out? How long?" he demanded, waving his cigarette in the air.

"It doesn't matter how long. We're not going anywhere. This is our home and this is where Bapuji is . . ." I faltered.

"Say it. This is where Bapuji is going to die," Bhai said. "And die not knowing the truth," he whispered, pointing a nicotine-stained finger at me.

"What would you know about the truth anyway? What truth do you represent, Bhai? Smashing somebody's head in with a stick isn't any kind of truth I recognize. Is that the truth you want me to tell Bapuji about? I've seen what's going on with my own eyes. If that's the truth, I don't want it," I said, spitting out the words.

"Don't talk to me with that holier-than-thou attitude, Bilal. Do you think that you're some kind of angel of righteousness? That you're above the blood and dirt the rest of us have to live in? You're not. You've just found another way to stare this horror in the face. You're just the same as us, the same as me. This lie is your hell, just as the truth out there is mine."

Bhai's words were like little razors cutting me in different ways. I saw myself in my mind's eye, stockstill, mouth open, stunned at my brother's words. He was standing there, dark eyes blazing like hot coals, his mouth making terrible shapes. Realizing what he'd just said, he held up his hand but no words came out. I wanted to go to him, to hold my bhai and tell him it would be OK and that we'd be fine. But I couldn't. Although there were only a few yards between us, they felt like a canyon, and we were standing on either side looking at each other over the divide. The fissure was too wide and too deep and the bridge across was burning.

Feeling tears stinging my cheeks, I brushed at my face and sucked in deep gulps of air.

"You're right. All that you say is true." My voice was barely a whisper. I pointed to the other room. "Go ahead. Bapuji deserves to know but I can't tell him. I've carried around this lie for what feels like an eternity. Do me a favor and put us both out of our misery . . ." I dipped my head and moved away from the entrance.

My brother took a step forward then stopped.

Do it, please, Bhai. Do it. I could sense his mind racing. He took another step and walked into the other room.

*

When Bhai emerged, his face was ashen and his eyes were no longer blazing but were dull embers. He grabbed me by the back of my neck and pulled me toward him, our foreheads touching. When I was a little boy, he'd lean toward me and I'd automatically stop what I was doing and touch my forehead against his. Attached to one another like two magnets, we'd both laugh. This time there was no laughter but we both smiled a little. Letting go, he walked quickly out of the house and slipped into the alley. I watched him go, a white shape flitting in and out of the darkness.

When I couldn't see my brother any more, I sat on my stool next to Bapuji's bed. Muttering in his sleep, he turned and opened his eyes.

"Bilal, I just dreamt your brother came to see me."

I pulled the cover tightly over him.

"It was only a dream, Bapuji," I replied.

"I thought it might be. He just sat here and stroked my head for a long while. Then he leaned in close and whispered into my ear."

"What did he say?" I asked resignedly.

"He said he was sorry," replied Bapuji.

"That's all he said?" I asked.

"That's it. What do you think he was sorry about? I tried to stop him to explain but he left," said Bapuji.

"I don't know, Bapuji, but I'm glad he came," I replied.

"Me too, Bilal," sighed Bapuji drowsily. "Me too."

Chapter 41
(3 days until Partition)

He saw me. I'm sure of it. Clutching the medicine to my chest, I froze. The streets were deserted now and only mobs roamed the alleys, burning people in their homes. I'd finally managed to make Rajahwallah open his door and give me some medicine when I'd been seen.

I ducked into an alley. *What is that?* A set of feet shuffled nearer. *Somebody's found me. If he keeps coming in this direction, he'll practically fall over me. I have to move. Now.* Taking a deep breath, I threw myself forward and began to run without looking back. Hearing a yell, I put my head down and started to sprint. I knew these streets well enough. *I'll lose him in the tangle of alleys sooner or later.* I took a left turn then a right then left again, trying to create some distance between us.

But he stayed with me, shouting things. "Run as fast as you can, little rat, but I'll still catch you."

I know that voice! Desperate now, I entered a maze of streets and feinted to go right but spun and sprinted left in the hope of losing him. Running down a dark set of alleys, I emerged and couldn't hear footsteps following me. In front of me were four alleys leading in different directions. Stopping and sucking in a deep gulp of air, I heard footsteps from the alley behind. *Choose, Bilal!* Taking a left, I sprinted down a long alley so narrow I had to shuffle sideways, slapping the wall with my hands to propel me forward. I shot out at the end into a square space and on all four sides were high walls. Running to one side, I looked up. *Too high!* I was trapped. I flattened myself against the wall. *Has he seen me go this way?* Sliding down the wall, I pulled my knees in and held them with my hands. I waited.

Seconds later he hurtled through the little opening and pulled up sharply. Seeing me in the corner, he smiled.

"Almost, little rat," he said, panting. "You almost lost me but I grew up around these streets." Straightening, he took a step toward me.

I stood up.

"What do you want with me?" I asked quietly.

"With you? Nothing. I want nothing with you or from you, little rat. What I want to do is remove you from the face of this earth, you Muslim scum," he hissed, almost spitting out his words. "You see, I know your brother and he's hurt my brothers. He's escaped me a few times already. When I heard he had a little brother, well, I knew it was a gift from the guru." He took another step forward. Producing a little bottle from his pocket, he looked at me and smiled. "You know what this is, little rat? It's oil." Digging into his pockets, he produced matches. "And you know what these are, don't you?"

Taking a step back, I looked at him in horror. Even after all I'd seen and heard, this was beyond anything I had expected.

"You're going to burn, little rat, and I'm going to hear you scream. Then I'll go after your brother and burn him too," he said. Coming closer, he flicked oil on to me, dousing my shirt completely. Then he began to laugh, match in hand.

"Don't do it," said a voice from the opening to the square.

We both turned to see Manjeet stride toward us.

"I'd never have found this place if you hadn't dropped your kara at the entrance," Manjeet said, producing a silver bangle.

The boy with the match looked at Manjeet in confusion.

"Sat Sri Akaal, brother, what are you doing here?" asked the boy.

Manjeet looked at me then back at the boy, and took another step. He was a lot taller than the other boy.

"He's my friend," said Manjeet quietly. "Put your matches away and leave. He's not part of your fight."

"But he's Muslim scum and his brother has hurt many of ours. This would be sweet revenge."

"No, leave here now," repeated Manjeet, taking another step to stand right in front of the boy.

Scowling, the boy retreated and growled, "And what if I don't?"

Manjeet stood perfectly still and pinned the boy with a look. "If you don't leave here right this minute, I'll take that bottle and douse your face with it and burn it off. Just your face. I swear on the guru, I will."

The hand that was holding the match trembled as

he glared at Manjeet. Reluctantly the boy put down his match.

"I know your brothers," the boy said. "What will they think when I tell them of this?"

"Tell them. You think they'll side with you? I'd be surprised if they didn't rip the beard off your face, you thug," said Manjeet angrily, throwing the kara at his feet. "Now get out of here before I get really angry."

The boy stepped around Manjeet, giving him a wide berth. Scowling at me once more, he disappeared from sight.

Manjeet turned to me and sighed. "Are you OK?"

I doubled over and vomited. Groaning, I leaned against the wall to steady myself. Holding my stomach, I blinked tears away from my eyes.

"No, not really, but I'm glad to see you, Manjeet," I replied breathlessly.

Slowly recovering myself, I stood up straight and looked at Manjeet. Neither of us said anything and an uncomfortable silence settled.

Don't say it, Manjeet. You don't have to say it.

"Bilal, I won't be able to see you any more. My family think ... that Muslims ..."

I felt anger flare up inside me.

"What about you, Manjeet? What do you think? You know me. I am not Muslims. I am Bilal. Just Bilal."

Clenching his fists, Manjeet set his jaw. "It's not that, I—"

"What is it then? What's the difference between you and me?"

"It's all changed, like you said it was changing. We shook our heads and laughed at you back then but it has changed. You tell me what the difference is. My family tells me I should join the struggle, that I should take a kirpan and . . . that I should burn people . . ."

"But what do you think? What do you say?" I asked desperately.

"It doesn't matter what I think!" shouted Manjeet, his face set in a grim mask. "Don't you get it, Bilal? You really think there's a choice in any of this? We're just kids. What choice do we have about anything? You think you're in control? You're not. No matter what you do, the choice has already been taken away from you. You might think you're in control—and sometimes you might be—but when it matters, when

261

it's important, Bilal, there is no choice."

"There is always a choice," I whispered. Looking at the storm-flared sky, my heart filled up like a sinking boat, sadness welling up faster than I could ship it out with my cupped hands. "You chose to come after me even though you knew it would cause you trouble."

"I'll always be your friend," replied Manjeet in a low voice. "We just can't be friends. I'm sorry. I have to go."

Looking directly at me, Manjeet backed away toward the opening. I watched as the orange turban I knew so well flickered and disappeared from view and drifted out of my life.

Chapter 42

(1 day until Partition)

The chairman of the market town committee, Ramprakash Gianwaral, stood outside our house shuffling his feet.

"I'm sorry, Bilal. For you, for this town. Your bapuji was ... is the finest man. And such a good friend," he said.

"Thank you for coming, Mr. Gianwaral. I'm sorry he isn't well enough to see you but I know he'll be ever so glad to hear you came."

"Yes, I hope so," he replied. "Bilal, there's this rumor going around that your bapuji ... How can I say it ... ?"

"Yes, Mr. Gianwaral, what rumor?" I asked.

"Well, that your bapuji doesn't know—or rather isn't aware of—er, the current situation. Is that true?"

I looked right at Mr. Gianwaral. He looked back at me steadily, neither of us willing or able to look away.

"Yes. It's true," I replied.

Mr. Gianwaral slowly shook his head. Scratching his beard, he produced a handkerchief and patted his forehead. The silence grew and settled like a heavy cloak between us. Folding his now moist piece of cloth into a little square, Mr. Gianwaral pocketed it and looked at the open door behind me. Clearing his throat loudly, he opened his mouth to speak but no words came out. Gathering himself, he stood up straight.

"Quite right too. The truth is for the living after all. Tell him . . . give him my best, Bilal. My very best," he said, turning on his heel.

"I will and, Mr. Gianwaral, is it true you're opening up a music room tonight? For a dance?"

"It's supposed to be a secret," he sighed, "but I suppose there are no secrets in this town, eh, Bilal."

"Is it true?"

"Yes, a few of us sad old fools thought it would be a fitting tribute to . . . to our last few hours as a united nation. To our India." The words, heavy and choked, escaped from Mr. Gianwaral's throat.

"I see," I replied.

"I would have liked your bapuji to be there but perhaps under the circumstances it's best he isn't . . ."

"No, best he isn't," I agreed.

Mr. Gianwaral took a step forward, put his hand on my shoulder and squeezed it. "Quite right too," he said, and walked away.

I should have kept my mouth shut instead of telling Chota about it when the two of us met on the rooftop. He immediately jumped up and literally dragged me onto my feet.

"I don't want to go, Chota," I mumbled.

"Why not?" he asked, excitedly hopping from foot to foot.

"Because Bapuji is close now, Chota. The town is on its knees and dying. The last thing I want to see is a dance."

Chota stopped jigging about and moved to the edge of the rooftop to look into the distance.

What can I say to him now that he knows what I'm really like? There's no more Saleem to lighten the mood, or Manjeet to keep everything calm. Just me and my misery.

"Look, Chota . . ."

"It's OK, Bilal, I don't really want to go that much. I just thought it would help take your mind off things leading up to midnight," he said.

Moving to stand next to him, I looked down at the desolate marketplace.

"There are only rats left in the market now. You can hear them skittering and squeaking when you walk past. Some of them are as long as my arm, you know," Chota said, holding up his arm and waving it at me.

"Just as well you've got short arms then or else I really would be worried," I replied, smiling.

Looking up, I gazed into the sky and realized that this would be the last time the sun would be going down on this India. Tomorrow it would rise on another India. One that was changed forever. "*But I'm still here, India,*" I wanted to shout. "*I'm still here.*"

"What time does this dance start?" Chota asked quietly.

"I heard it's going to begin just after the sun goes down and will stop before midnight," I replied. Making up my mind, I put my hand on Chota's shoulder. "OK, I think Doctorji is going to visit soon so I'll leave him a note asking him to watch over

Bapuji and to let him know we'll be back before midnight, then I'll come with you to the dance."

Beaming, Chota nudged me in the ribs. I tried to cuff him but as usual he was too quick and moved out of my reach.

Chapter 43

That evening, Chota led the way, the bounce in his step propelling him forward. *Always forward with Chota.* Looking over his shoulder, he kept stopping and waiting for me to catch up. As soon as I caught up, he'd move on again. I was in no hurry to go anywhere, especially not to a music room where we were unlikely to be allowed in.

The music room was on the other side of town in a grand old house owned by a former nawab. The house had seen better days but tonight golden light streamed through, bathing the white building, bringing it to life. Hearing noises filter through the open windows, I stopped walking. Chota turned round to look at me enquiringly.

"Maybe we need to hold back for a few minutes

until we're sure we can get in without being seen?" I suggested.

Chota sniffed. "If we wait, we'll miss the beginning, Bilal. If I can show you a way in that nobody knows about, will you come?"

Looking from Chota to the house, I pursed my lips. Knowing Chota, he probably did have a way into the house that nobody knew about. Then again it was just as possible he was lying.

"OK, but try to be quiet," I replied.

We skirted around until we were at the back of the house. The gentle rustling of the large trees surrounding us reminded me we were away from the main town. Chota signaled to me to duck down and we crawled on all fours until we were directly under a window.

"We can get in this one," said Chota.

"Are you sure?" I asked skeptically.

Without waiting, Chota stood up and lifted the window. It creaked open partway and then stopped. Chota scrambled through and I heard him land with a dull thud on the other side. Standing up, I ducked under the window and tried to pull myself through. Chota hadn't realized that I was at least twice his size and there was no way I was going to get through. He looked at me and grinned as I hung there glaring down at him.

"I'm stuck, Chota! The window needs to be pushed up a little," I said, wheezing.

Chota clambered on to the little ledge and started pulling the window up but it was stuck. I realized that I couldn't move backward or forward.

"Chota, I can't get back out either. You'll have to inch it up. What if we both try together?" Chota readied himself to leave.

"One, two, three ..."

The window flew up with a sharp sound as I crashed into Chota and we both landed heavily in the dusty room. Untangling myself from him, I rolled to my feet. *Somebody must have heard that!* I turned to the window and closed it as quietly as I could then pulled Chota toward a long window with a thick curtain. Shoving him behind it, I wrapped the heavy material around us and waited. Footsteps entered the room and moved toward the window. Holding my hand over Chota's mouth, I stood statue still. Finally, the footsteps receded and we came out from behind the curtain. Listening carefully, we slipped to the door. The hallway was empty as I followed Chota down it toward the light. I pulled Chota into a dark alcove and ducked down.

"That looks like the main entrance to the room. We need to get upstairs and see if we can look down on to it," I whispered.

Chota nodded and sped off. At the end of the hallway was a staircase. We made our way up slowly as faint sounds of the tabla filtered through to us accompanied by soft sitar strings.

"I think it's about to start," I said.

On the first floor, a thin layer of dust had settled on everything. Silvery light filtered through each room we passed. Somebody had clearly thought the house needed airing out for the occasion and all the windows were open. Sheer drapes floated in the silence as we raced through the eerie old palace. We came to a little stairwell leading a few steps down. At the bottom was another door that looked as if it hadn't been used for years. Walking through it, we faced a large, square grille looking down on to the music room. Chota turned to me and smiled as if to say, "*I told you so,*" and leaned against the wooden frame. Moving to stand next to him, I looked through one of the grilles at the brightly lit room.

A large square of crimson cloth had been laid down in the middle of the high-ceilinged chamber, on which pillows and cushions were strewn. On these sat the men of the market town committee. There was some gentle chatter but the mood was somber. Nobody in the room had forgotten what night it was and the weight of history settled on the assembled audience like a thick layer of dust. In front of the audience there was a small, black square of material—the performance space. Lanterns lit up the whole room and each committee member had his own diva. The whole room danced with flames flickering in time to an unheard beat. Two musicians sat to one side of the black square on cushions. Dressed smartly in white, waiting, they both looked tense. The tabla player flexed his fingers in readiness and the sitar player distractedly made last-minute adjustments to his strings with well-practiced movements.

The kathak dancer appeared from behind a long drape. Dressed in shimmering white, she glided to stand in front of the audience with a handful of rose petals. Strewing them on the ground in offering, she gently tipped her head at the audience in greeting and stepped back, the ghungroo bells on her ankles chiming softly. Silence filled the empty spaces of the music room, broken only by the whistling wind and the rustling drapes that delicately whispered an introduction for the elegantly poised dancer.

The sitar player began to strum, sending out plucked sounds that soothed the audience. Caressing the strings back and forth with his fingers, the sitar player sent out sounds to fill each corner of the room. The dancer stood perfectly still, chin tilted down, eyes closed, listening to the reverberations pulsing from the strings. Closing my eyes, I heard what she heard, but what did she feel? Plucking one string then another, the sitar player alternated the sound and, my eyes still shut, I heard the first tabla thrum ease alongside the rhythm set by the sitar player, followed quickly by another thudding beat. Slipping into a pocket of silence created by the sitar player, the tabla set upon a rhythm.

I looked at the two musicians. They were friends. Like me and Saleem, like me and Chota, like me and Bapuji. Friends who left a space for their loved ones to occupy. Loved ones who knew when to speak and when to stay silent.

The music continued and then there it was. A jingling, jostling sound. I looked through the trellised window as the kathak dancer slowly moved her feet, rustling the many ghungroos attached to her ankles to meet the tabla sound. Another pocket of space created by her friends. Three different areas of sound now existed and filled the space in between our ears and minds. The diva flames flickered to meet the sound, swaying in tribute to the dancer's slapping feet. Moving in time to the music, the dancer raised her hands. Spreading her arms, she emulated the wingspan of a bird and floated back and forth, flying on the currents of music. Right arm then left moved as she mirrored the flight of an orange-breasted kingfisher, all the while moving her feet. Subtly the music changed, and suddenly she was a silverside fish gliding through the water. The sitar mimicked the sound of water gliding over pebbles and the tabla thrummed gently in the background, imitating a fish diving in and out of water. Chota was mesmerized, his eyes reflecting the swaying diva lanterns and the dancer in brilliant white.

The tabla player increased his tempo and then suddenly stopped, fading into the background as the sitar introduced another scene. Watching the dancer's gestures, I noticed the shadows playing on the wall behind her. She was telling a story. Of India and her beginnings. Of her rivers and her mountains. She was a fish reveling in the fresh waters of the Indus River then an eagle soaring over the high Himalayan peaks. At times she was the land and at other times she was the air but there was no mistaking that she represented Mother India. Raising her elegant neck, she moved it left and right, long tapered fingers making shapes before our eyes. All of us in that room watched her history unfold. Our history. The first settlers on the banks of the rivers, the first hunters, the first dancers. Rudimentary instruments made with the soil and wood of the land spinning to the same rhythm of the present, the span of years forgotten by the slapping feet on the earth. Her earth. She was a tree, a banyan. Arms spread out, branches springing from the ground obstructing one other as the tabla beat introduced branch after branch, leaving no trace of beginning or end.

And now she was a monsoon, gestures swirling in the soft light. The tabla leapt to meet the dancer's urgent movements and the sitar instantly set after it.

The sound of slapping feet and tinkling bells echoed around the old house like the splashing sound of raindrops on the hard earth, fingers tracing droplets in the air. The tabla increased in sound and something else. Fury. The sitar strings made a harder, clipped sound now. Taking a step forward, the dancer swiveled on her heel and began to spin. The drumbeat became harder and quicker and the spinning increased in speed. The monsoon was descending and the people braced themselves for the impact. All eyes were on the dancer's swirling skirts, the hem spreading wide and encompassing the land. Eyes fixed on the dancer, my vision swam as the spinning continued, blurring the scene. The flashing white figure bled into the darkness. I could feel the gale force of the monsoon through the grille. The golden lights flickered, buffeted by the brutal wind. And still the spinning continued.

I saw the moment when I first climbed the banyan tree with Bapuji. The time I fell and Ma dabbed at my knee with her sari. The first time Saleem and I drew water from the well. The time we discovered the rooftop and made it our own. The first time Bapuji took me around the market stalls with him. The first time I sat and listened to the monsoon rains outside our house. The first time I tasted a sweet mango. The first time we swam in the river and caught fish for our dinner. The first time I realized Bapuji was really sick. The first time I decided my life would be a lie.

The dancer suddenly stopped spinning and slumped to the floor, head bowed. Just as abruptly the beat stopped. The dance had ended.

Chapter 44

We moved from shadow to shadow, edging our way back home from the old palace. There was excitement in the air and something else. Fear. We watched as people took to the streets in celebration—or was it confusion? Sounds of joy mingled with the silence of the departed. People stood and watched, waiting for the clocks to strike midnight. I could understand their confusion. *Will we feel differently? Will anything change? What will tomorrow bring?*

There were many who stubbornly refused to acknowledge that anything was going to change and just as many who felt this was the dawning of a new era for India. I was buffeted with all these mixed emotions, my own and those of the people of the town. Clinging to the shadows, we froze as a large group of men with torches stomped past.

"India for ever!"

"Jai Hind!"

I could feel Chota's hot breath in my ear.

"They're still burning people in their homes ..." he whispered breathlessly. "Bilal, you're hurting my arm."

Blinking, I realized I had been gripping his hand tightly. "Sorry," I replied.

"We'd better get you home," said Chota.

Turning to face him, I looked at Chota, puzzled.

"Your house is nearby—we'll go there first," I replied.

"No, no, I'm coming with you to your door just in case something happens."

"Chota, if something happens it could happen to either of us. I'll be fine."

Turning his head to look out on to the street, he grabbed my arm.

"Let's go," he said, taking my hand and leading me away.

I shook my head. Secretly I was pleased Chota was coming with me. I knew it was selfish but I was scared and the last thing I wanted was to be alone.

Skulking through the streets, we approached our school and Mr. Mukherjee's house. Chota was moving on briskly but I pulled him back.

"Chota, wait. I just want to see Mr. Mukherjee quickly," I said. "He asked me to let him know if I was OK a few days back. He's probably worried."

"OK, but make it quick. We can't hang about here," replied Chota.

Knocking, I peered through the cracks in the door for any signs of life.

"Mr. Mukherjee? Mr. Mukherjee? Hello . . . ?"

Silence. *Where can they be?* Chota stood twitching impatiently. Suddenly the heavy wooden door creaked open and Mr. Mukherjee's long arms reached out and pulled me into the house, quickly shutting the door behind me.

"Wait, wait! Chota's outside," I cried.

Opening the door again, Mr. Mukherjee called for Chota and bustled him inside the house.

"Bilal, where on earth have you been? I went to visit your bapuji and Doctorji was there fretting about you. He said you'd left a note explaining you'd be back later."

"Do you know if he told Bapuji he didn't know

where I was?" I asked.

"I don't know but I doubt it. Your bapuji was sleeping, he can barely raise his head ..." said Mr. Mukherjee.

"I just needed to be away for a while," I said quietly.

"Bilal, it's not safe to be wandering around these streets. Half the town is celebrating and the other half has left. Then there are those who are roaming the streets ..."

"I know, we saw them," I replied.

Mr. Mukherjee blew out his cheeks and sighed. "Get home, Bilal. He was asking for you."

"OK. Let's go, Chota," I replied, turning to the door.

"Wait, I'll come with you," said Mr. Mukherjee, pulling on his coat.

"No, Masterji, you'd better stay with Auntie-ji," I replied.

"Auntie-ji will be OK by herself, Bilal," said Mrs. Mukherjee, emerging from the dark.

Putting her arms around me, she wrapped me in an embrace. Still holding myself rigidly, I didn't put my arms around her. As much as I wanted to, I couldn't. Stepping back, she smiled sadly.

"You're braver than you'll ever know," she said.

Bowing my head, I stared at my feet.

"I had always thought bravery was having the courage to tell the truth. I'm a coward but that's OK. I can live with being a coward if Bapuji can die in peace. Mr. Gianwaral said something earlier today that made a lot of sense. He said the truth was for the living."

Stifling a cry, Mrs. Mukherjee turned away, covering her face with her scarf. I knew she didn't want me to see her crying. Leading her back into the dark room, Mr. Mukherjee turned to us.

"Wait here, I'll be back in a minute," he said sternly.

Chota hovered near the window impatiently.

"OK," said Mr. Mukherjee, returning. "Keep moving. Even if somebody cries out for you, keep walking. If we're stopped by one of these mobs, you're both my sons and we're going to celebrate in the main square. Is that clear?"

Chota and I mumbled in agreement and we set off walking briskly through the streets. There was little or no light in some parts and we did our best to keep up with Mr. Mukherjee's long stride. Approaching my street, I caught up with Mr. Mukherjee and walked beside him. As usual he was muttering to himself. Turning to me, he smiled nervously. We reached our front door and stopped. Looking around to see if we'd been followed, I knocked. Waiting a few moments, I knocked again and pressed my ear against the door to listen for signs of movement. Hearing footsteps advancing from the other side, I stepped back.

"Who is it?" asked a gruff voice.

"It's me, Bilal," I replied.

The heavy door opened and Doctorji quickly ushered us all into the house.

"Bilal, where have you been?" he asked angrily. "Your bapuji has been asking for you. What were you thinking? He's close now and . . ."

Mr. Mukherjee held up his hand and Doctorji stopped talking.

"He was with me. I wouldn't let him leave. I felt it wasn't safe on the streets so I kept both of them at my house," explained Mr. Mukherjee.

Looking from me to Masterji, the tension left Doctorji's shoulders and he bowed his head. He put his hand on my shoulder. I tried to see his expression but he looked away, obscuring his face in the half light.

"Go to him, Bilal. It's almost time," said Doctorji, his voice barely above a whisper.

My legs felt as if heavy bags of rice were attached to my ankles. Dragging one foot forward and then another, I shuffled toward the wall of books. Three sets of eyes burned into the back of my head and I turned to see three very different faces. Mr. Mukherjee stood with his pocket watch in hand, knuckles white from gripping it too tight. Doctorji looked right through me into the darkness over my shoulder, eyes glazed with sadness. Chota stood nearest me, little fists clenched.

"Please, I would like to be alone with Bapuji for his ..." Choking on the words, I turned away so they couldn't see my face.

"Are you sure you don't want us here, Bilal?" asked Mr. Mukherjee.

"Yes. I'm sure. Please take Chota home, Mr. Mukherjee," I replied, recovering myself slightly.

"I'm not going anywhere," said Chota stubbornly.

"Listen, son, it's not safe out there. I'll walk you home and you can come back tomorrow," said Mr. Mukherjee, leading Chota toward the door.

On the threshold, Chota turned to me once more.

"I'll be here if you need me, Bilal. Just call my name. I'll be here," he cried and scampered into the night.

Still he won't leave me. Feeling my throat constrict, I blinked rapidly.

I heard Mr. Mukherjee swear under his breath but Chota was already gone.

"That boy ..."

"He'll be OK, Mr. Mukherjee," I said. "He's always OK."

"We'll meet later," he replied and, raising his hand in parting, he walked out through the door.

Doctorji stood rooted to the spot, his face a grim mask. *They are both so different,* I thought. Bapuji always reminded me of the roots of a banyan tree—layer upon layer of overlapping tendrils shooting off in different directions. Doctorji was the opposite. He reminded me of stripped bamboo—upright, unbending and almost impossible to break. *This must be difficult for him too, they've always been best friends.* Moving to him, I held his hand and squeezed it.

"I'll let you know first, Doctorji. After it's ... happened," I said quietly.

As if waking from a dream, Doctorji looked down

at my hand entwined with his. Closing his thick fingers around mine, he squeezed hard, almost making me cry out. Letting go suddenly, he walked away and, without turning, closed the door behind him.

Chapter 45

I walked past the wall of books and stood at the foot of the bed. Doctorji had lit a candle and placed it by the bedside. The golden flame threw flickering shapes around. As I approached the candle, I noticed my dark shadow painted on to the sand-colored wall. *Are you a witness then? Have you come to see for yourself if I can go through with it?*

Sitting on the bed, I watched as Bapuji slept, ragged breaths wheezing through dry, cracked lips. Fetching some water, I dipped my fingers into the glass and gently wet his lips. I put my hand on his chest and closed my eyes. Each breath was a struggle. A battle for air. A war against himself. Bapuji's chest was barely rising. It was a war he was going to lose.

Opening his eyes unexpectedly and looking right

at me, he smiled.

"It's you," he whispered.

"Doctorji's gone, Bapuji," I replied.

Fighting to keep his eyes open, Bapuji chuckled.

"I am too, almost," he said quietly.

Feeling for his hand, I clasped all my fingers around his frail bones and held it close to my chest. We were both spinning in the candlelight. Midnight was minutes away as I held on to my threadbare dreams. Bringing Bapuji's hand to my lips, I kissed it, hot tears winding down my face and falling into the darkness over the edge of the precipice.

"Bapuji, we're almost there . . ." I said, leaning in close to whisper into his ear.

"Bilal," replied Bapuji.

Tell him. Tell him now before it's too late. All the webs I had spun in my mind were unravelling. Each knot was coming undone. *Tell him! Tell him!*

"In less than a minute, Bapuji . . ." *I'm a liar!*

"My boy, it's difficult to speak . . ." he whispered.

The clock struck midnight. Sounds of celebration, anguish and sadness erupted from the direction of the town square.

"Did you hear that, Bapuji? That sound . . ." *This is*

forever my burden. Forever. "India is free," I cried.

"Bilal, dear heart ..." said Bapuji, his voice barely carrying to my ears.

Leaning even closer to hear, I cradled Bapuji's head in my hands and kissed his forehead.

"Bapuji ..."

"You are my India," whispered Bapuji.

The sounds from the town square continued as Bapuji's breath became more ragged, coming in short, sharp pulls of air. Suddenly, one long, last gasp escaped his lips. A whistling breath of air purer than all the rest.

The candle still flickered, chasing shadows across the wall. Looking over to the wall of books, I noticed that a few heavy hardbacks had been pulled out. Holding Bapuji close to my chest, I wondered how many you'd have to pull out until the whole wall would collapse.

Chapter 46

The noise of the town was closer now but different. The sound was angrier, more furious. I could hear screams and shouted insults, but in the darkness of our room with the guttering candle, it felt far away. There was a crash and a thud at the door. Somebody was trying to get in. Holding Bapuji close to me, I rocked back and forth, stroking his hair. I'd done it. He'd died in my arms not knowing the truth. He'd died with his beloved India still whole. I'd done it. The banging continued but it didn't matter to me. Although I was afloat in the darkness, my heart felt like it was sinking. Then suddenly there was the sound of splintering wood.

A voice pierced the quiet gloom.

"I told you, didn't I, little rat? I told you I'd burn

you. India will never be free until we get rid of vermin like you. Who's going to save you now? Burn!"

A part of my mind heard a bottle smashing on the hard earth in the other room. The wall of books burst into flames first, the fire hungrily consuming book after book. Spreading steadily along the wall, the fire took to the ceiling and reached for the charpoi. There was more shouting outside and sounds of a struggle.

"Bilal! Bilal!" *I know that voice. How can my aunt be here?* "Bilal! Can you hear me, Bilal?"

"You have to get out!" cried another voice. One I knew so well. *What is Bhai doing here? I told him not to come back. It doesn't matter now anyway.*

Somewhere in the back of my mind, I realized that the candle had finally guttered out, but by now the whole wall was on fire and bits of old leather and yellowed paper floated in the air. All around us, bits of knowledge burned, crumpled paper blackening then dissolving into a fine charcoal powder. Reaching out a hand, I tried to catch a few pieces of floating paper but each fragment crumbled at my touch.

Closing my eyes, I held Bapuji closer to me, sighing as the warmth from the blaze lulled me to sleep. I'd done it. I'd kept my promise to myself and now I just wanted to rest.

Into that peaceful silence came another crash and a figure emerged from the darkness.

"Bilal, we have to get out. Now!"

"Bhai, what are you doing here?"

Grabbing me roughly, he pulled at my arms.

"No! I can't leave Bapuji. I can't," I cried, clinging on to the body next to me.

Letting go of my arms, Bhai knelt down in front of me.

"Bilal. He's gone. And in a few minutes, you will be too. Let him go," he said.

"I can't, I can't. I couldn't tell him at the end. I wanted to but I couldn't," I said quietly.

"Let him go, Bilal. He's no longer suffering." Taking my hand, Bhai slowly pulled me close and held me in his arms. "Let him go, Bilal," he whispered into my ear.

The fire was everywhere now and Bhai stood up. Snatching the bed sheet, he ran to the water bucket in the corner of the room and doused the sheet. Bringing the bucket back, he poured it over me. Then throwing the sheet over both of us, we took a step forward. The wall of books had mostly collapsed and blocked our path.

"We have to jump through it, Bilal! Are you ready?" Bhai shouted.

"Yes!" I cried, gripping his arm.

Taking a few steps back we ran up to the wall of flame and, closing our eyes, crashed through. Tumbling through to the other side, we landed hard. There was fire all around us and I felt a pain in my ankle. Bhai stood up and dragged me through the door. We fell into the cool night, desperately gasping for air.

Bhai helped me up as flames and smoke swelled above us. Bits of paper floated into the night sky and spread in all directions over the market town. Chota stood near me with a rock held tightly in his fist and next to him stood Bapuji's sister. She looked from the house to me in horror. Her mouth made shapes but no words escaped. Reaching out, she pulled me toward her and wept. She smelled of jasmine. Eventually, moving away from her, I went to stand next to Bhai. We watched the raging fire shoulder to shoulder, tears making tracks down our grimy faces as the death of Bapuji gave way to the birth of a new nation.

After a while, Bhai turned to me. Grabbing me by

my shirt, he pulled me close in a rough embrace. Burying my face into his chest, I held him tight. Then forcibly pushing me away, Bhai took a step backward. I saw the fire reflected in his eyes, so similar to Bapuji's. *Don't leave.* There was a crushing pain on my chest as he walked away and disappeared from sight.

That very night, Bapuji's sister took me away from the market town to start another life. That was the last time I saw Bhai. I don't really even remember what he looks like anymore, but I've never forgotten how his dark eyes blazed like hot coals when he was angry.

Epilogue
60 Years Later

A hush descended on the assembled crowd as I finished speaking. I looked out over a sea of faces staring up at me. The silence stretched on, filling all the empty spaces in the air. I looked at the deep blue night sky, shimmering stars peppered haphazardly across the large expanse. When the invitation to celebrate sixty years of independence had arrived, urging me to visit the market town, I had been horrified. My whole adult life had been spent trying to forget what I'd done but I had never truly been able to escape the past.

In my professional life, my instincts had led me to become a lawyer. *A defender of the truth.* My many years of service had finally elevated me to the exalted position of Chief Justice. *Who better to spot a liar than a liar himself?* The market town committee, seeing my name in the newspapers, had invited me back to tell my story. Eventually, I had convinced myself that I needed to confess to the town, and the thought of finally unburdening myself after all these years was tempting.

Well, I had told my story—all of it—but the silence of the crowd was deafening.

Sniffing, I could smell something in the air. Twitching my head this way and that, the smell triggered an old memory in me. *Monsoon is coming.*

The crowd still had not stirred. Picking up my piece of paper, I crumpled it into a ball and gathered my stick. The town mayor looked from the crowd to me in confusion and moved forward to help me. This was not the story he had been expecting. I waved him away and teetered off the stage. Addressing the crowd, the mayor broke the spell of silence by thanking me for coming. The crowd began to stir in the market square but a strange quiet still hung in the air.

At the side of the stage, I found an upturned barrel and sat down on it. Another memory tugged at me, of Mr. Pondicherry and his favorite barrel in the shade. "In this barrel," he would say, "is contained a sea of stories." *He had a story for any occasion*, I thought, chuckling to myself. Standing on stage for such a long time had left my legs cramped and stiff. Rubbing them gently, I tried to bring them back to life.

As I sat there, a steady stream of people started to gather around me. They came in groups and individually. Slowly but surely, they came. Some touched my feet in blessing and others shook my hand. Mothers, fathers, sons, and daughters all came. Old men, watery eyes shimmering, shook their heads and patted me on my back, reliving the past through my words. Friends and family of those in my story smiled in remembrance, thanking me gratefully. Many just touched the hem of my kameez and moved away quietly while many others cried softly and stood near me. Looking around at people's faces, I felt the weight of my burden become heavier. I had hoped that by telling my story I would feel better. Relieved. Instead it felt as if the revelation would bear me down.

From the corner of my eye, I noticed a young boy hovering on the edges of the crowd. *He looks strikingly familiar.* The crowd slowly began to disperse and when everyone had finally left, he shuffled closer, head bowed respectfully.

"Bilal-ji, I heard your story. It meant a lot to me. You see, I'm Doctorji's grandson."

Ah. That was it. Such a familiar face.

"My bapuji's name was Bilal. My name's Gulam," he said.

"Gulam was my bapuji's name. It's an honor to meet you, son," I replied.

"No, no, Bilal-ji, what are you saying? The honor's all mine," he said, shaking his head and bowing down to touch my feet.

"Your grandfather taught me a great deal," I replied.

"I still miss him. He stayed in the town and continued working as a doctor until he died. He continued visiting the local villages too."

"Of course he did," I replied, smiling. "He said he would. Doctorji was a man of his word."

"Bilal-ji, please can you wait here? I wasn't sure you were coming today so I didn't bring it with me. Please will you wait here for me? I'll be right back."

"Of course, I'll be right here," I replied.

Making myself comfortable, I leaned against the wall. The town had changed little. The market still stood with all the alleys and backstreets still intact. If anything, it seemed a lot bigger now and attracted much trade from all parts of the country. *Bapuji would have been pleased.*

Gulam returned, breathing hard and doubled over, clasping his knees.

"Stand up, son, you'll get your breath back quicker that way," I said, remembering myself when his age.

He looked at me curiously and stood up. "I was always running from place to place and Grandfather used to say that to me." Gulam produced a crumpled envelope from his pocket. "When my bapuji died, as his only son I was responsible for organizing his possessions. Going through his files, I found a large box of Grandfather's things and in it was this envelope. It said *To my good friend Bilal* on it but I wasn't sure who it was for. Until now. Perhaps because you left abruptly he never forwarded it to you but I think it's right you should have it."

Taking the envelope from him, I froze. Looking up at Gulam's curious expression, I turned the letter over in my hand. My heart quickened and the stars in the sky seemed brighter, sharper. Opening the letter carefully and unfolding it, I gasped. It was a letter from Bapuji dated August 14, 1947. My eyes swam as I tried to focus on the scrawl in front of me. The first

299

few lines looked as if they had been written by a child, the letters oversized and strangely spaced. What followed was a bolder hand written in a flowing script. *Bapuji must have tried stubbornly to write the letter and when his strength gave out, somebody else must have taken over.* I looked up at the young boy, my hands trembling. *Doctorji.* Forcing myself to look at the letter, I began to read.

Dear heart,

Of all the things I wanted to do before I died, the most important was to write you this letter. I am proud of many things, Bilal, but I am proudest of being your bapuji. I couldn't have asked for a more courageous boy and knowing this, I know you will be an even greater man.

I don't even have the strength to finish this letter but Doctorji is here helping me. My boy, he told me about your oath and the lengths you've taken to keep the truth from me. Dear heart, what did you take upon yourself?

Bilal, you are my India. You are my dream. What you have done, the gift you have given me is branded on to my heart. When you receive this letter, please realize that when I found out, I cried, not in misery but in joy knowing I had a son like you. I beg you not to blame Doctorji for telling me. The righteous old fool felt he had no choice. I know that you of all people know how that feels.

Please tell Rafeeq I am proud of him too. Despite our arguments, tell him I have never forgotten him. I hope he finds peace both in the world and in his heart.

I will end this letter now. The thought of leaving you is too painful. I leave you my most prized possessions, my books. I know you will look after them. Perhaps every time you pick one up, you'll smile and think of me.

Bapuji

Hands still trembling, I stared at the letter. A few minutes passed and the words became lines and shapes, memories, and pictures.

"Bilal-ji, are you OK?" asked Gulam, concern etched on his features.

Folding the letter carefully, I placed it in the envelope and clutched it tightly. In my other hand, I still held the crumpled piece of paper I'd had on stage with me. Smoothing it down, I tried my best to flatten the edges. Curious, the tall young man with Doctorji's serious face looked at the piece of paper.

"Everybody lies," he said, reading aloud my hastily scrawled prompt.

I handed him the creased paper.

"Bilal-ji, what shall I do with this?" he asked.

"Whatever you like," I replied and moved past him. "It no longer belongs to me."

Glossary

Anaar Gully Hindi for "Pomegranate Alley"

aseel a bird bred specifically to take part in cockfights

Assalamu alaikum. "Peace be upon you." A greeting used by Muslims throughout the world

banyan a vast fig tree with many roots, traditionally used as a meeting place or as shade for meditation or teaching; the national tree of India

bapuji common Hindi term for *father*

bhai common Hindi term for *brother*

bhen common Hindi term for *sister*

chai common Hindi term for *tea*

chapati a flat, round bread cooked on a griddle

charpoi a portable string bed

chota common term used to describe children; used in this context by Bilal and his friends to describe Chota as the "little one" or "shorty"

chuppal a simple type of footwear, like sandals or flip flops

daal lentils; a popular dish in India

dacoit common term for *bandit*

dhoti traditional men's garment, worn wrapped around the waist and legs

diva a small oil lamp that is lit and placed around the home; it has a single wick and is usually brightly colored

ghungroo a musical accessory tied to the feet of classical Indian dancers, consisting of small bells and cymbals

guru a Hindu or Sikh religious leader

imam a leader of congregational prayer in a mosque; also a religious teacher or leader

"Jai Hind" "Victory to India" or "Long live India"

ji a form of address for elders, strangers or anyone meriting respect; example: *Doctorji*

Kabir an Indian poet, mystic and philosopher (1440–1518)

kameez a traditional Indian shirt

kara an iron bracelet which serves as a reminder for Sikhs to follow the morals of their faith

kathak one of the eight forms of Indian classical dance, originating in northern India

kirpan a sword or dagger worn by many baptized Sikhs at all times

lassi a yogurt-based drink, similar to a smoothie

ma common Hindi term for *mother*

maidan a large open space often used for playing cricket and for meetings, etc.

masterji common Hindi term for *teacher*

monsoon seasonal winds that bring heavy rainfall to all of India

"Namaste." "I bow to you" or "My greetings." A greeting used by Hindus throughout the world

nawab a Muslim prince or landowner

pandit a wise or learned man in India; often used as an honorary title

peepul a tree that is traditionally revered in India

sari the traditional dress for mainly Hindu women, worn wrapped around the waist and draped over the shoulder

"Sat Sri Akaal" "Blessed is the person who says 'God is truth.'" Used by Sikhs throughout the world when greeting other Sikhs, regardless of their native language

sitar a stringed instrument that is plucked; Predominantly used in Indian classical music

tabla a popular percussion instrument used in Indian classical music

Tagore, Rabindranath a famous Bengali poet, novelist, musician and playwright (1861–1941)

talwar common Hindi and Punjabi word for *sword*

Map of India, 1945, before Partition

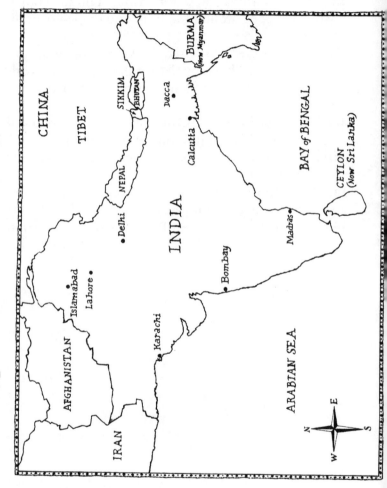

Map of India & Pakistan, 1947, after Partition

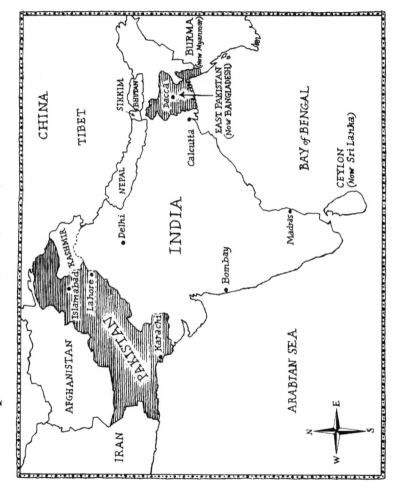

Some Historical Notes
from the Author

August 14, 1947 saw the birth of the Islamic Republic of Pakistan, a nation state separate from the predominantly Hindu India. Pakistan was made up of two regions: West Pakistan on the Indus River plain, and East Pakistan, which is now known as Bangladesh. At midnight the next day—on August 15, 1947—India won its freedom from British colonial rule.

The break-up along religious lines resulted in the movement of about 14.5 million people—Muslims going to Pakistan from India and Hindus and Sikhs going in the opposite direction. Many people lost family, friends, and homes, with communities cut in two during the upheaval. It is estimated that over 1 million people died in the violence during this period.

Although it is over sixty years since Partition, conflict between India and Pakistan continues to this day, with large-scale communal violence still occurring. The far-reaching and often devastating consequences of Partition on every aspect of Indian and Pakistani life are as evident today as they were on the stroke of midnight on August 14, 1947.

Irfan Master